By: Bernard Jamar Haynes

Dedicated to Estella Hayes & Mary Collins Barnett.

Jamar-James Independent Publishing ISBN*: 9781718098053*

Chapter 1

It's the summer of 2003, and it's a beautiful day in New York City. Manhattan: it's rush hour. The city is filled with yellow cabs driving in all directions. Most people in the city prefer taking cabs rather than wasting gas in their own cars; many don't even own cars. Most of the workforce in the city lives elsewhere. New Jersey, upstate, some come from as far as Philadelphia. One of the most expensive areas to live in the city is Park Avenue: let's face it; you have to be making big money if you live on Park Ave. Most cannot afford it-unless you're the Thomas Family. Allen Thomas makes more than five hundred grand a year. He's a big-time lawyer. He's a partner in a firm he started with some others. Allen sometimes gets tired of the city life in New York. His wife, Tiffany, is a Doctor. She works at a local hospital. Allen and Tiffany have three kids. Kevin Thomas, their oldest son, is a typical seventeen-year-old. He makes average grades and loves rap and heavy metal. Jenny is fifteen years old. She is into books and is a straight-A student. She wants to be a lawyer like her father. And then there is the little one, James (sometimes referred to as little Allen/Allen because of his striking resemblance to his father). He's a seven-year-old doing what seven year old boys do. They live in a five-room condo in Manhattan. The typical upper middle-class working family in America you could say.

"I want those files on my desk this afternoon, Todd. No exceptions." said Allen.

"I will have it done, Mr. Thomas." Allen's new hire is fresh out of law school. Allen is not trying to cut the rookie any slack. "Just make sure you're at the meeting today at ten." said Allen. It was the norm at the Thomas law firm. Allen Thomas called all the shots. Although he was the CEO, he often touched base with his employees. Some considered him a prick that kissed ass to get to the top. Allen did not care. He was making money and living the life he dreamed of. That evening after work, Allen met Tiffany at the grocery store.

"Hey honey, how was work?" asked Tiffany.

"The same old," he replied. "You know I have another new kid fresh out of law school. He's a total fuck up. Book smarts, but no common sense."

"Oh really? I mean, give him a chance honey, you were not the best when you started out," Tiffany suggested.

"True, and I learned the hard way because of it. He's also black. He's my first black hire at the law firm," Allen said, shaking his head.

"Are you serious?"

"Yeah, I know. With this affirmative action shit I had to hire him. Just my luck he will rob everyone at the damn firm blind."

"Well I guess the world is trying to change, honey. Maybe he is one of the good ones." "Good ones?" said Allen with a laugh." "Yeah, you know, like Oprah." Allen scoffed. "Oh ok, yeah...let's hope so."The couple talked more about their day as they shopped for groceries. They soon made their way home to their condo on Park Ave. Meanwhile at home their son Kevin was at the house blasting music not knowing his parents were seconds away from walking in.

" Living the life as a thug until the day I die, yeah, this is my song." sang Kevin.

"Turn that mess off or I'll tell mom and dad you listen to rap." replied his sister.

"Man you're just like them. Just because they raise us to be racist does not mean we have to be racist. You need to wake up, Jenny."

"'Wake up?,'" she repeated. Are you forgetting that a nigger robbed me last week?"

"That was one person--you cannot fault the whole race for one person. And don't use the N word around me: it's bad enough mom and dad use it unconsciously," said Kevin as he turned Tupac up on the stereo.

Suddenly there was a key in the lock. Allen walked in first.

"Turn that trash off this instant, young man. Damn monkey music." "You were raised better, Kevin." added his mother.

"Man you guys are a terrible. I'm out."

"Where are you going? Dinner is in a hour." yelled Allen to his son. Kevin ignored his father, then headed out to his friend Derrick's house. Derrick lived in Brooklyn in the projects. The two boys met at their performing arts school in the city and became fast friends. Allen hated the fact that his son's best friend was black.

"I swear that boy doesn't listen to anything. Then if I take the BMW away from him I'm the bad guy." said Allen.

"I don't know what's wrong with him. Since he's been hanging out with Derrick, he's gone crazy. He thinks he's black." said Jenny.

"He needs to go to a military school. That will straighten him out." added Allen.

" Oh now Allen, it's only a phase." said his wife. Tiffany prepared dinner while Allen turned on Fox News

"A woman is beaten and raped while in her home. Witnesses say the suspect they saw leaving the apartment complex running away on foot, was an African American male, but there are no leads yet." said the news reporter.

"See? These people are animals. My dad was right--take them all back to Africa."

"Where is James?" said Allen. "He's in his room asleep, dad. I picked him up from school earlier." said Jenny.

Later that evening the family, along with James, sat down to dinner without Kevin. Allen almost always dealt with work calls at home. It seemed the law firm could not make it without him.

But he did not get a call this night. The family ate, and then everyone was back into their own personal lives. Jenny went to the mall with her friend Samara. Tiffany took James to the store. Meanwhile Allen stayed at home doing paperwork in his home office. He tried to put out of his mind the fact that his son was not conforming to his ways. Sometimes Allen felt bad about the way he viewed blacks, Hispanics, or any other race that was not Caucasian. But it was the way he was raised. On top of that he watched too much television. He believed everything derogatory that he heard about people of other races. He never took the time to get to know people from different cultural backgrounds.
An hour into work Allen heard his son Kevin come in.

"Anyone home?" yelled Kevin. "Have a seat, man," said Kevin to his friend Derrick. Derrick sat on the love seat in the living room as Kevin went to grab his book bag. Allen walked into the living room. Allen had heard much about Derrick but never actually met him.

"Dad, this is Derrick." said Kevin.

Derrick stood up with his hand out. Allen did not shake his hand but he gave a quick hello, then called his son into his office.

"Son, what's your problem? You bring strangers into our home."

"Dad, chill out man, we came by to pick up some CDs then we're out. Be honest—you don't want Derrick here because he is black."

"Now son, it's not like that, but how can you forget that your sister got robbed last week by one of them."

"Listen to you, dad. Look: I'm not like you and mom, ok? And I never will be." Kevin stormed out of his father's office, grabbed his CD's, and he and Derrick left.

Allen was furious. His son was out of reach, he thought. Allen went back to his office to finish some paperwork. He ended up falling asleep in the office and was awoken by his wife.

"Honey, its eleven thirty. How long have you been in here?" "Is it that late, honey?" he said as he kissed his wife. The two went to bed.

An hour into sleep the phone rang. Tiffany answered.

"Hello," she said. "Hello, this is Langston."

"Hey Langston."

It was Allen's brother Langston. Langston lived in Virginia. Langston was partners with his brother in the law firm. He ran the southern office.

"I was just calling to let you guys know Grandpa Thomas is selling the house. Is Allen in?"

"Yes, hold on one second." said Tiffany. She handed the phone to Allen. "Hey, what's going on; do you know what time it is Langston?"

7

"I'm sorry, but Grandpa Thomas is selling the house. You know the house in Spotsylvania, Virginia. It sits on about two or three hundred acres of land. Man, there's horses; cows; it's beautiful. He is selling it all. But he said he would rather give it to you and the family. Grandpa Thomas always loved you the most Allen." said Langston.

"Man, that's a beautiful house. I have not seen it in some years. Is it still intact?"

"Yes, he keeps in top shape. Several families were looking into buying. Let me know the status by next week."

"I'll do that." "Good night."

Allen hung up and told his wife the news. His wife was delighted to hear the news. They had wanted to move out of the city for years.

"Honey, so are we going to make the move? It would be great for the kids." said Tiffany.

"The city life has already corrupted Kevin. He's hanging out with thugs now. He thinks he's one of them," replied Allen.

"And I will be damned if Jenny comes in the house with a black guy for a boyfriend, over my dead body."

"Well, times are changing. My coworker Tonya is black and she is a very good person. They're not all like that."

"What the hell are you saying? Kevin has been rubbing off on you, I see? Two niggers killed my uncle Jeff when they robbed him 5 years ago. Did you forget that?" Allen said with raged.

"They are all the same." The couple fell in silence and soon drifted off to sleep.

Chapter 2

Saturday morning Allen was up early. He had some work to do at the office. When he got there, the paperwork from Todd was on his desk. Allen read over the cases. It was very good for a kid fresh out of law school, but by any means Allen wanted to find something wrong with Todd's work. He found two paragraphs that were not indented and called Todd, even though it was a minor error. When Allen had first started, he had made far more mistakes than Todd. Lawyers will make minor errors initially when starting in their first practice.

It was eight in the morning on a Saturday. Todd's phone rang several times.

"Hello Todd, is that you?"

"Yeah, who's this?' said Todd. "It's your boss. Why the hell aren't these fucking paragraphs indented on these cases?" Allen said.

"Sir, I must have forgotten; I'm sorry." "Forgot? What the hell; I do not pay you to forget. Get your ass in here and fix this shit." Allen slammed the phone hanging up. As he did so he mistakenly hit speaker at the same time. "I swear these monkeys are all the same," he said.

Suddenly he heard Todd's voice.

"Excuse me sir," he said. Allen's heart skipped a beat. Todd had heard the racist comment.

"Uh, nothing, Todd. Just, uh, do not worry about it I will fix it; see you Monday."

Allen hung up the phone. Throughout the day he wondered if Todd would go above him to their HR department and even further to the EEO representative.

Meanwhile, Todd could not believe what he had just heard. He made it his mission to talk to Allen about it Monday morning. He had experienced problems with racism while in the Navy Reserves. But he never said anything; he let it pass. Not this time, he thought.

Todd called his father to discuss the issue, still feeling shocked by his boss's comments as he listened to the phone ring.

"Hello, Todd Sr. speaking."

"Pop, hey, this is Todd."

"Hey boy, what's going on?" Todd explained,

"My boss and I got in to a slight argument on the phone over some errors I did on my reports." His father replied,

"Well, if you made errors take responsibility and fix them, son."

"That's not all, Pop. When we ended the conversation he said, and I quote, 'I swear all these monkeys are the same'."

"Are you fucking serious?" his father fumed.

"Call your EEO rep ASAP at your human resources department. There's no place for that nonsense in the workplace."

" Yeah, Dad, that's what I was thinking. This is crazy--my first week on the job and this happens."

"Everything will be ok, son."

After their conversation with his father Todd felt somewhat better, but was still disturbed by Allen's remarks.

When Allen got home, he told his wife what happened.

"I mean, I was talking out loud. Then I hit the speaker when I slammed the phone on the hook," he explained.

"Allen, you can be fired for something like that," said his wife. Allen scoffed.

"I am the law firm; my name is on the building. Come on now," he said with a laugh.

"Well, you have heard of the NAACP. A lot of black people use their services when involved with discrimination cases," said Tiffany.

"We will be ok, honey."

Just then Kevin walked in. He was dressed in a Rocka Wear denim outfit with a New York Yankees fitted hat on that was slightly turned to the side, and Timberland boots. He also had headphones on.

"Life is a bitch and then you die that's why we get high" said Kevin, quoting a lyric from a Nas rap song. Allen snatched his headphones off.

"You won't listen to that ghetto crap in my house anymore." Kevin shook his head and went to his room, slamming the door behind himself.

"And do not let me see you dressed like you're about to rob a liquor store again, boy," Allen yelled. "I swear I will not stand for my son to act like what he is not."

"Allen, it's only a phase; it will pass," said his wife. "I sure hope so," he replied.

"Well, honey, some of the guys and I am going to play golf this afternoon at this course in the Hamptons. Mr. Marshall, our Partner and CO CEO, is a member there. I will not be back for dinner, but leave something out for me."

"Sure honey," said Tiffany. Allen got his clubs and changed clothes. His friend Robert came to pick him up.

Back at the house Kevin and his mother talked.

"Mom, you and dad have to get out of the sixties. African Americans are not all the same. You cannot fault the whole race for some people that have made mistakes."

"Yes, I understand you honey, but your father and I are from the South. We were raised differently. I admit there are some good black people, but my thoughts of them as a whole just cannot change overnight."

"I cannot live like this." "I know son. The city is corrupting you."

"What are you saying?!" yelled Kevin.

"First off, watch your tone with me, young man. And second, your father and I are thinking about moving the family down to Virginia."

"Mom, come on, I have one more year in high school. And what about the friends I've made?" Kevin was furious--he loved New York City. It had been his home for his entire childhood.

Suddenly, Jenny came in from gymnastics practice.

"What's all the yelling about?" she asked as she kissed her mother on the cheek. "I was just telling your brother about the possibility of our family moving to Virginia.

"Virginia, mom--are you crazy?" said Jenny.

"Look, I'm not going to argue with you two. It's not final anyway, but when it is you two have no choice. Now I'm going in to work for a couple of hours I will be back before three." She kissed her children and headed off to the busy NYC Medical Center.

"This is bullshit!" Kevin kept saying aloud. And for once his sister agreed with him.

"Yeah, what am I going to do in the country; how will I be able to shop?" said Jenny. The two children sat in the living room mad at the world. James was in his room watching TV; he heard the commotion but was too busy watching Spongebob to worry about it.

Later that evening, the family sat at the dinner table. Allen had made it back in time for dinner. While at the table he noticed the gloomy faces.

"What's up guys, why the sad looks?" said Allen.

"I told them about us possibly moving to Virginia." said Tiffany.

"Well, I will have you know that we are going to move out of this city. You know a branch of my law firm is in Virginia. And honey, you can easily get a job at the local hospitals down there. If that takes some time we have plenty in our savings until you start back to work."

Tiffany arose from the table and kissed Allen on the cheek. She met Allen in college at NYU. They happened to be from the same county in Virginia. She had always dreamed of maybe one day moving back home.

"Baby, I did not know you wanted to move this fast, but I cannot wait to get out of this city." said Tiffany.

"I wanted to surprise you," Allen replied. "As a matter of fact, I planned for you and I to go visit the house next Sunday. Kevin, you and your sister and brother can stay here."

Kevin got up from the table and went to his room.

"That boy will change soon enough. I swear the city has destroyed him."

"Dad, where is Virginia?" said James.

"It's down south, son. You will love it." Tiffany suggested,

13

"Maybe we can take James with us? It will give Jenny and Kevin some time to themselves."

"That sounds like a good idea honey," replied Allen to his wife. Jenny ate the rest of her dinner and went to her friend Ashley's house, while Kevin sat at his desk in his room on his cell phone, telling Derrick the news that he would be moving south.

It was a pretty quiet weekend at the Thomas home. The older two children shut themselves away from their parents, while James did not really know what was going on. Although James was young, his father often told him to watch out for the black children in school. They would steal his lunch or his coat. But James found himself playing with kids of all races in school. Sadly, if his dad knew of that he would have thrown a fit.

Soon the weekend was gone, and it was Monday morning. As soon as Allen got to work he was called down to the Equal Opportunity rep. Allen was prepared, knowing that Todd would have said something. He walked in to the Equal Opportunity office and discovered Todd sitting at the desk with John Davis. John was the head EEO rep that Allen hired eight years ago.

"Hello Allen, it's not every day that I get to talk to the head of the firm. Is your brother still running the branch in Virginia?"

"Yes, he is. Can we get to the point? I have a busy schedule."

"All right. Todd came to me this morning about a phone conversation he had with you this weekend. He said he felt you used a racial remark. He said you made this remark, and I quote-these monkeys are all the same-."

"First, I apologized to you, Todd. I didn't mean you or your race. I had already hung up with you I was talking about something else. You caught the tail end of the conversation."

14

Todd sat there burning with rage. He knew what he had heard, but he also knew Allen was the CEO of the firm, and didn't want to risk losing his job. He had just bought a house, and had a child on the way. So he played along with it."

"Sir, I'm sorry, I must have heard wrong." said Todd, feeling like an Uncle Tom.

"Ok. Is that it? I have several meetings today." Allen said as he headed to the door."

"Uh, I guess so sir," said John. Allen shook Todd's hand quickly and headed back to his office.

Damn that was a close one, Allen thought to himself. The rest of the day at work Todd could not think straight. Should he resign? Or should he take the case higher, and sue the law firm? Later that day at the gym Todd met up with his friend Antonio. The two young men discussed what had happen to Todd. Antonio and Todd met in Navy boot camp in Chicago, and had been best friends ever since. They consulted each other for advice often. After their talk, Todd decided to put the incident behind him, and move on. The rest of Allen's day was filled with meetings. In most of the meetings Allen addressed the fact that he would be taking over the other branch of the firm in Virginia. Allen had always spent time at the Virginia branch. When he was gone, Mr. Marshall would run the

firm in New York. It really would not be a big change for him, except that now he would be living there in Virginia.

The rest of the week he took off calling area schools for his children. It was April as they continued their plans to make the move after the kids got out of school for the summer. Kevin and Jenny were still extremely upset about moving. Kevin spent most of his time with his boy Derrick. When the weekend came Kevin went to Brooklyn to see his boy. He took

15

the subway, about a thirty minute ride, since it was a nice spring day in the city. As Kevin came up the subway steps, there were two men robbing a young woman for her earrings.

"Give them up bitch," shouted a masked man with a gun pointed to her head.

"What you looking at white boy?" said the other man, who was also wearing a ski mask.

"Nothing man." said Kevin.

"Give up that iPod, white boy."

Kevin feared for his life and gave up his iPod quickly. The two men jumped in a Jeep Cherokee and sped off. The girl ran away screaming, calling the cops on her cell phone. Kevin's heart was racing. He headed towards Derrick's house which was in the heart of the 'hood in the Brownsville area of Brooklyn. Derrick was standing outside his housing project waiting for Kevin.

"Damn, man, what's wrong with you? I know you're white but you looking pale as a ghost," said Derrick with a laugh.

"I just got robbed man. These two dudes were robbing this girl when I came up the subway steps. Then they robbed me for my iPod.

"Damn man, these cats out here are animals, man. That's why I carry heat wherever I go, man." Derrick pulled up his shirt showing his chrome nine.

"I told you to call me so I can meet you. If these cats don't know you they will rob you, man. Plus, you're a white cat, man. They see that as even more of a reason to rob you. They figure you got a black girlfriend that lives out here. And some cats hate that, they're not as open minded as you and I."

"It's all good man, I will be ok. Man, let's go to the city." said Kevin. The two young men got back on the train and spent the day in Times Square. Kevin was hoping that his dad

16

would not ask him what happened to his iPod if he did not notice him using it. Allen paid

three hundred dollars for the iPod and would be furious if he knew two black men for it

robbed Kevin.

Chapter 3

Back at the house, Tiffany was already beginning to pack some things. Allen talked to his brother and assured him that he and his wife would be down on Sunday afternoon. Jenny was away at a friend's house until the evening, while James. Sat in his room playing his PlayStation. Allen had everything in order. Now the only problem would be taking his brother's word about the house. He was hoping everything was intact like his brother told him. Allen's grandfather had told him that the house was built in 1825 and that it had been the Thomas home for some generations now. Allen and his wife couldn't wait to see it. At five am on Sunday Allen, his wife, and James left New York and headed for Virginia. As they left, Allen told Kevin and Jenny to take care of the house. The two teenagers promised to do so, but in the back of their minds they had thoughts of a house party.

It was a long 8-hour drive for the Thomas family. Tiffany drove as far as Delaware; then Allen drove the rest of the way to Spotsylvania County. James slept almost the entire ride. When they arrived, Allen went to his brother's house first, just ten miles down the road from the house that Allen and his family would be moving into. Langston's house was a nice brick house where he and his wife Cristina were raising two boys. Their younger two, ten-year-old twins Mark and Luke was in the yard playing when Allen pulled up in the driveway. James jumped from the car to go play with his cousins, while Allen and his wife went in to talk about the house with Langston.

"Yeah, it's in good condition. You know it's been in the family for four or more generations." said Langston.

"I always loved that house. As a kid I dreamed of it being mine one day." replied Allen.

"Well, how about you and Langston go check the house out and Tiffany and I will prepare dinner." said Langston's wife Christina.

"Yes honey, we can look at the house together again before we leave," said Tiffany.

The two brothers agreed. It was about a ten-minute ride to the house, and when they pulled up in front, Allen was amazed. It was beautiful. He had always imagined living there when he would visit his grandparents as kid. After gazing over the land, the two brothers entered the house.

"Damn, this house is huge," said Allen.

"It's one of the biggest houses in Spotsylvania County." said Langston. The fifteen thousand square foot house was fully furnished. Allen's Grandfather had decorated his home with the finest antique furniture money could buy.

"You know Grandpa Allen always wanted to keep the house in the family. Too bad he is getting senile now; his Alzheimer's is getting worse. Just last week I had to tell him several times who I was before he came down to see me. He hates being in that home we put him in last year. Anyway, look around. I'm about to go outside to dump some trash." said Langston.

Allen walked around the beautiful mansion. He went upstairs to the bedrooms where there were six rooms, all of which were already just as fully furnished as the rest of the house. He went to what would be the master bedroom. As he walked around the bedroom suddenly he felt a cold draft as the door slammed. Allen was startled for a second. The windows were closed. He shook his head then walked out the room. Allen then went to the master bathroom. As Allen relieved himself, the half open bathroom door slammed again.

"Langston we are not kids anymore you can quit slamming doors." Allen said with a chuckle.

"What?" He heard his brother yell from downstairs. He met his brother in the kitchen.

"Man, I was in the master bedroom and suddenly the door slammed. Then the same thing happened when I used the bathroom"

"Oh it's probably just a draft."

"Yeah, you must be right." said Allen.

"An old house like this is usually drafty," Langston reassured his brother.

The two men looked around the house a little more, then headed back out to the truck.

"Langston, I must say it's a beauty. I cannot wait to move in." said Allen.

"How are the kids taking it?" asked Langston.

"Well, Kevin's taken it the hardest; he's caught up in that hip hop trash. He hangs out with thugs. I've got to get him out of the city. Jenny does not want to move either, but I'm sure she will adapt quicker than Kevin. And James is just seven so you know he will be fine he can make new friends."

"Yeah, I figured Kevin would be the biggest problem. Hell, he and Jenny can finish up high school at Robert E. Lee Academy. It's a mostly white school. A couple of blacks and china-men, but he won't be corrupted like in New York City." said Langston,

"Thank God." Allen felt a sense of catharsis as they drove back to Langston's house. When they arrived, their wives had the kitchen smelling good. Aromas of pot-roast, macaroni & cheese, string beans, and corn bread were in the air. The family sat down to eat Sunday dinner.

Back in the Big Apple, Kevin and Jenny were home alone. They sat in the living room watching T.V. and debating if they should throw a party or not.

20

"I don't know, Kevin. Mom and Dad will be back Monday night. What if we make a mess?"

"Chill out, Jenny, we will have plenty of time. We might as well have fun while we can. We will be going to live in hick town in a couple of months." said Kevin.

"Yeah, Dad said that he already has plans to transfer our records to a school there.

"It's all your fault. You just had to go and get black friends. You know how Mom, and especially Dad, feel about it." said Jenny.

"That's the problem: you, Mom, and Dad are living in the past. You've got some nerve--you have posters of Aaliyah on your wall."

"She was not like the rest of them." "You got it twisted. In all races of people there are good and bad. One day you will see the light," said Kevin as he opened the refrigerator door. Jenny shook her head at her brother then turned the T.V from Fox News to MTV.

"Hey, my boys are coming over later to play Halo."

"Why are you telling me? You're the oldest."

"Because they're black and I do not need you telling Dad." As Kevin said that he handed his sister twenty dollars to keep her mouth shut.

Later that evening, Jenny went to the mall with some friends while Kevin and his boys played Halo on the XBOX. When Jenny got back home she and her friend Lisa walked into a house that seemed more like a club.

"Go shorty its ya birthday," yelled her brother.

Jenny turned the stereo off.

"What the hell are you doing," said Kevin, as he turned the stereo back on and a notch up more on the volume.

"I'm not listening to this trash," said Jenny.

21

"Trash," said Derrick.

"Chill, I got this," Kevin told his friends. Kevin grabbed his sister by the arm and took her to his room.

"Look, I do not need you embarrassing me in front of my boys." "You mean hoodlums," replied Jenny.

"Whatever, it's midnight. Now I could tell dad you're way past curfew or you can shut up and do your girly things with Lisa."

"Ok, I got it," said Jenny. Kevin went back out to the living room, while Jenny and Lisa went to her room.

All their friends left around 2 am. Kevin and Jenny had school the next day, and their parents would be in late that evening, so they figured they had plenty of time to straighten the house out. They invited friends over to help them clean up after school.

Spring break was in a week, but since they knew they would be moving in the summer, and transferring schools, the two wanted to spend as much time with their friends as they could.

As Allen drove across the George Washington Bridge, he could smell the city air.

"From the smell of the country air to this--I cannot wait to move." said Allen.

"I just hope the kids will adjust ok, said Tiffany.

"Trust me, when they graduate from college, they will thank us." said Allen. "I guess you're right, honey."

They had about twenty more minutes before they arrived at their home on Park Avenue. James was sound asleep in the back seat. Allen had planned to rent out their Park Avenue home. That would be extra money to play with in stocks, Allen thought to himself. Soon they were back home. The house was clean. Kevin and Jenny greeted their parents and kid brother at the door. James was still sleepy, so Jenny laid him down, while Kevin helped with the bags. When Kevin got downstairs, his father was pulling suitcases from the trunk.

"Kevin, how are you son."

"I'm ok. How was the trip?" asked Kevin.

"The house is amazing. Your room is almost the size of our living room here. I think you will like it. If not, in time you will learn to like it. Change is good." said Allen.

The two headed up to the house. Later that day, Allen went over moving dates and also confirmed dates when Kevin and Jenny would start at their new private school. The young teens dreaded the news but they knew it was coming.

Throughout the remaining months into spring, Allen used the time to clean out his office. He also had several meetings to close out the spring court cases. Soon, Allen had everything in place to leave. His wife Tiffany had already transferred to a hospital in Virginia. The family was set to move at the beginning of summer once school was out. Soon the day came to move, moving trucks arrived at the Thomas home in the early am on a Saturday morning in June. The movers did all the hard work while Allen and his family packed small items to take with them on the drive. Allen, his wife, and their youngest, James drove in the BMW X5, while Kevin and Jenny drove in Kevin's BMW 3 series. Tiffany's Audi A8 would be shipped.

It was a 10-hour drive due to a major traffic jam on 95-South. They arrived a little after three in the afternoon. Jenny was astonished when she saw the enormous house she would now be living in.

"Wow, this is not a house, it's a mansion. Dad, you did not say the house was this big." said Jenny.

"I know I wanted to surprise you." Tiffany smiled at her husband.

"Maybe Jenny will adjust quicker than we thought," Tiffany replied. Kevin got out of the car and walked around the house. Kevin noticed that there was a basketball court about fifty feet away from the house.

"Let's go inside guys," said Allen. He picked up James. The family entered the house. Jenny ran upstairs to claim her room.

"I hope you know I got the biggest room." Kevin yelled. James ran upstairs following his sister.

"I want a room too," he screamed. Kevin sat down at the kitchen table. "Why don't you go check out your room, Kevin?" said his mother.

"I'm ok, I'll check it out later."

"You need to drop the attitude, young man, and get used to this home." Kevin then got up and headed up to see his room.

"That boy will learn sooner or later that we make the rules." Allen replied. "He will be ok, given some time." said Tiffany.

"The moving truck should be here soon. We did not have that much stuff since this house is already furnished. They better be on time," said Allen. "You know how those niggers are though; they will probably be late." Tiffany said with a chuckle.

The movers were right on time. By nine that night the family already had most of their stuff unpacked, since for the most part they left their condo fully furnished. Allen ordered pizza for dinner.

Kevin was still pissed at the fact that he had left New York City and left some good friends behind. Jenny was upset but happy to have a bigger room. After dinner the two older children sat on the porch.

24

"We do not even know what this school is like. Dad kills me, putting us in a school that we know nothing about." said Kevin, not realizing his father was standing in the doorway.

"First of all I have researched the school and it's the number one private school in Virginia. So suck it up boy," Allen said in a loud voice. Kevin shook his head.

"It will be ok, Kevin. I'm mad too but we have to make the most of it. We can make new friends. And you will be going off to college in a year anyway. You would have been leaving New York sooner or later," said Jenny, trying to make her brother feel better. Kevin decided to go to bed early while the rest of the family stayed up a couple of hours playing Monopoly.

Around ten o'clock Tiffany laid down James for bed. Allen went around the house closing all the windows. He did not want the hot air to interfere with the central air system. The family laid down for bed. James had trouble sleeping in his new bed and after an hour of sleep James awoke to use the bathroom. When he went back to his room, the window was wide open. There was an extremely cold draft in the room. Allen moved a chair towards the window to stand on so he could look out the window. The backyard stretched on for several acres. In the moonlight, James saw people in the backyard, all seemingly doing something to the grass. One of them was a woman with little girl by her side. The little girl looked up at James. Allen closed the window and jumped into bed, pinching himself to see if he was dreaming. As he lay in bed unable to sleep, James wondered why all the people he saw were black.

James climbed into his sister's bed as he always did when he was scared. The next morning James told his sister what he had seen, but she assured him that he only had a bad dream. James had told everyone by noon that day but they all reassured him that it was only a nightmare. Even though no one believed him, James knew it was not a dream.

Chapter 4

The family finished unpacking. They were done by late that afternoon. Later that evening Allen's brother Langston came over with his family for dinner. Langston's oldest son Greg had come home for the weekend. Greg was in the Marines. Langston told Greg to talk to Kevin and make him feel at home. After dinner Greg and Kevin went to a local bowling alley.

"So it's a big change from the city, huh." said Greg.

"Yeah man, I'm trying to adjust. You know how my dad is: everything has to be his way."

"Yeah, I know, he was always so stern. I noticed when I would stay with you guys in the summer. It will be ok though man, I mean, you can come stay with me on the weekends at Cherry Point. There are a lot of single military girls," said Greg.

"I don't know, man, we will see."

"James is getting big," replied Greg.

"He still acts like a little baby. Last night he claimed he saw people in our backyard last night. He said they were ghosts," Kevin said with a laugh.

Greg dropped the bowling ball on the ground.

"You ok, man?" said Kevin.

"Yeah, it must have slipped." Greg was shell shocked for a second, remembering seeing the same thing when he would stay the weekend with his great grandparents not too long before his grandmother passed away. He knew exactly what James had seen. No one had believed him either, not even when he told his parents. So he kept it to himself and did not tell Kevin, thinking Kevin would laugh at him if he told him.

"Little kids say some crazy shit sometimes," said Greg. The two young men bowled an hour or so. Then Greg dropped Kevin off.

As Greg drove to his parents' house, he reminisced on his youth. He had always thought the Thomas House was haunted. He had seen some crazy things in that house. He then turned up his radio to clear his head. When Greg looked back up there was a man in the road. Greg slammed on the brakes, but it was too late—he hit the man. Greg got out of the car to see if the man was alive and walked up to the body. When he attempted to touch the man to ask if he was ok, the man disappeared before his eyes. Greg jumped back and leaped into his red mustang 5.0 and sped off. When Greg got to his parents' house he packed his bags to leave. While packing, his dad walked in the room.

"You're leaving early son."

"Yeah Dad, I forgot I got a formation in the morning."

"You're a staff sergeant now; you can be late, can't you?" asked his dad.

"No, I have to be there, Dad."

"Why are you sweating so?"

"I went for a jog," Greg said.

"In khakis and a polo sweater? Whatever you say son, " his father replied. "I'll see you soon then. Your mother's asleep and so are your brothers. Take care, son."

Langston hugged his son. Greg was on I-95 South in no time. He wanted to get as far away from the old Thomas house as possible. Greg believed that James may have stirred up the same ghosts he would see when he was a child.

The Thomas family were preparing for bed. Allen and Tiffany had work in the morning, and the kids had school. Kevin's chore was to dump the trash before he went to bed. Kevin hated dumping the trash; he felt his sister should do it sometimes too. The dumpster was about eighty yards from the house. Kevin took the long stroll. Luckily the trash bag was not too heavy. The dumpster was right next to the basketball court. Kevin picked up the ball and took a couple of shots. Suddenly he heard a voice.

"I'd leave if I was you." said the voice. Kevin stopped shooting.

"Who said that?"

The voice started laughing. Kevin looked around, but there was nobody in sight. Kevin ran back to the house and told his father. Allen went to the dumpster with his son with his shot gun in hand. He did not hear or see anything.

"Boy are you sure?"

"Dad, I know what I heard."

"Maybe it was some kids playing. I would not worry about it."

The two men headed back into the house and Kevin went up to bed. Although still a bit spooked Kevin thought his dad had a good point. It was probably just some neighborhood kids. Allen was getting together a plan for a meeting he and his brother would have at the law firm in the morning, while Tiffany did Jenny's hair for school. James was already in the bed. Kevin pondered on the voice he heard but soon he was fast asleep.

In another hour the whole family was asleep.

James awoke to use the bathroom as he always did. He was so glad not to be wetting the bed anymore. His room was on the other side of the house away from the other five bed rooms. When he finished he headed down the hall to his room. Suddenly he heard a voice.

"Hey," it said. James was now in front of his room door. He was frightened and did not want to turn around.

"Hey, is it alright if we play," said the voice. James turned around. It was the little girl he had seen in the yard.

"I have to go bed," James told the girl in a scared and very timid voice. The girl walked closer to James. She touched his hair.

"Your hair is so different than mine," she said. James backed away.

"I'm so sorry please do not tell, I do not want another whipping," the girl said.

"I won't tell," said James. "Can I see your room?" she asked.

James pushed open his door and the two children walked into the room. They sat down at James's Fisher Price table. James was still very much scared. The little girls beautiful dark skin shined as the light from James's nightlight gleamed on her face.

"Why you are so scared," said the little girl.

James pointed to a mirror that was on the door. The girl had no reflection. She looked real to him and he felt her hand when she touched his head.

"Are you a ghost," asked James. She nodded her head yes.

"But I will not harm you. Look out the window."

James stood on the chair to look. The girl was taller, so she could see without standing on a chair.

"That's most of my family out there."

He was amazed that the sun was shining outside but still dark in his room.

"What are they doing?" Asked James. The girl laughed.

"You're silly boy; they're working. That's all we do from sun up to sun down. Master Thomas will not have it any other way." She said. "That's my mother there," and pointed to a woman.

James was confused; he did not know if he was dreaming or not. He was only seven, but was soon to be eight in three months.

"You sure have a nice room. It's nice in here. I snuck in. I had to get a break from the heat. I have been picking Tabaco all day."

James handed her a clean cold/wet towel to wipe the seat off her forehead. "Why thank you sir. "How old are you sir?" She asked.

'I'm seven. I'm not a sir yet."

"Yes but Mama says that I must call any white people sir or ma'am." James was once again confused.

"Well, I have to go back to work. Thank you for the cloth. Would it be too much to have some water?"

James took the girl down stairs. He poured a glass of Sprite. She took a sip.

"What is this? I never taste anything this good." James laughed.

"It's only Sprite.

The little girl tried to pronounce Sprite but she had trouble.

"My Great-grandma met a master's wife that taught her to read. She taught me some words."

"How old are you?" James asked. "I do not really know. My mama says I'm either nine or ten." Once again James was confused. He thought everyone had a birthday and knew their age.

"What's your name?" James asked.

"My name is Estella. Well, thank you for the drank. I have to go back to work."

James shut the refrigerator door. The door hit Estella in the back and she screamed.

"What's wrong?" James asked.

"My back!"

Estella then showed James her back. Estella's back was scarred severely from several whippings she'd had. When James saw her back he took two steps back and then puked on the floor. Estella fixed his clothes.

"Are you ok? Let me clean that up." Estella grabbed a towel from the stove then cleaned up the mess.

"You're different," said Estella. "But I must go. Master Thomas will kill me if I do not get back to work."

James walked her to the door. It was weird to him. In the house it was dark as if it was night time but when he stepped on the porch it was sunny and hot. James watched as the girl ran to her mother. Estella told her mother Mabel about James.

"Mama, a little boy treated me so nice in the house." Mabel cut her daughter off.

"Girl, I told you about sneaking in the big house getting water. Do you want to get lynched like your father?"

"No Mama," replied Estella. " Now get back to work little lady." Mabel kissed her daughter.

Estella picked up her bag and began working alongside her mother. Estella did a quick wave back to Allen who stood on the porch looking.

"Girl who are you waving at?" said Mabel.

"The boy on the porch." stated Estella.

"Girl there is no one on the porch. Get back to work if we finish early master may give us some extra food. Last week when we finished early he gave us that good left over ham."

Estella did not understand why her mother could not see the boy. It was obvious that he was standing on the porch. James walked into the field where men and women were working hard. James almost bumped into one man but as the man swung his hoe it went right through James's arm not touching him. James said excuse me to the man. The man did not reply as if he did not hear or see him. James saw hundreds of men, women, and children working hard in the hot sun. Then he saw a man that resembled his dad but older. The man came along riding a horse. He stopped in front of a man that was resting in the shade.

"Get back to work Nigger!" the man said as he jumped off the horse.

"Master, I was just resting a little," said the man, while scrambling to his feet.

The man snatched the hoe from the man's hand and smacked him in the face with the metal bottom part of the tool. The man fell to the ground, blood oozing from his face. Blood hit James in the face as well from the impact. The master began beating the man. James was terrified. He ran into the house and shut the door. The house was still dark as if it was night. James ran up to his room and jumped in the bed, pulling the covers over his head.

33

James wondered why the others did not help the man. They all continued to work as if nothing had happened.

When James woke up he ran to the window. The field was empty. Had he been dreaming, he thought to himself? As he went to wake up his sister he noticed blood on the floor. He ran and told his sister everything; he even brought her in the room to show her the blood, but it had disappeared. Once again James was told he had a bad dream. James thought to himself that from now on he would keep everything to himself. He was tired of people not believing him.

Chapter 5

Early Monday morning the kids were downstairs eating breakfast, while Mom and Dad got ready for work.

"First day in a new school, guys! I'm sure you all will have plenty to talk about this evening, and James I'm sure you will like second grade," said Allen.

In less than thirty minutes, the family was off. They were now in a new life, in a new town, in a new home. James adjusted well on his first day in a new school, just as his parents had hoped. He missed his friends from his school in New York, but was ready to meet new friends. James loved interacting with other children. He, unlike his parents, didn't see race as a factor when playing with other kids. Throughout the day at school he could not get Estella off his mind. He hoped that she would visit again.

Kevin hated his new school. He was getting stares from everyone the whole day and hated the fact that he had to wear a uniform to school. He could not wait to see his sister at lunch. Kevin thought that if they both complained enough, their father would let them go to a public school. But in the back of his mind Kevin knew his father would not move them to a new school. In between classes Kevin stopped to make sure his locker combination was right.

"Where is the fine arts class?" said a female voice. Kevin closed his locker. He saw a beautiful girl in front of him.

"Oh, I'm so sorry I was talking out loud," she said.

"No, it's cool, I have the same class. Maybe we can find it together," replied Kevin.

"I'm Daesha, by the way," she said. "Uh, I'm Kevin."

The two walked the halls. Finally, they found their class just before the tardy bell rang, and Kevin sat next to her.

After class, they had a ten-minute break before their next class. They went out to the campus park and chatted a little.

"So you're new here?" asked Daesha.

"Yes, uh, I'm from Manhattan. This is my senior year. My dad hated us living in the Big Apple so we moved here."

"Damn, from New York City to this," said Daesha."

"Well, I'm from Richmond. I went to a public school there for the past three years, and then my mom moved here to Spotsylvania. She had been saving for some time to get me in this school."

"Yeah, this school is expensive," said Kevin.

"So you always offer black girls help to find their class?"

"What's that supposed to mean? Yeah, I mean, if you were purple I would have offered." said Kevin.

"Purple! I don't know if I'd trade in my skin for that," she said as the two laughed.

"It's just that you're the first white student to speak to me today."

Just then Kevin's sister walked up. She stared at her brother shook her head and kept walking.

"You got a problem?" said Daesha.

"That's just my sister, sorry. Look, calm down maybe, we can exchange numbers."

"No, I'm good," said Daesha said as she walked away. Kevin chased down his sister.

"What the fuck is your problem Jenny?" yelled Kevin.

"Now you want to date them?! Dad is going to have a fit."

"Look, we were only talking. You need to chill out, plus even if I were to date a black girl you better not say anything. And I swear, if you even mention it to Dad you will regret it." Kevin's tone was so harsh Jenny thought twice about telling their father. Kevin went to class and totally ignored his sister the rest of that day in school.

After several meetings at work and meeting some of the new lawyers that Langston hired, it was about two pm. Allen decided he'd go home early. He could finish up his paperwork later. He had about twenty-five cases that his law firm was handling. Allen had already reviewed seventeen of them. On the way home, Allen took a shortcut. The only thing was that he had to drive through Sojourner Square. Sojourner Square was a predominantly black neighborhood. It was a faster route, but he hated driving through Sojourner. While at a stop light just before leaving the neighborhood, a black Hummer pulled alongside Allen's car. Sounds of loud rap music blasted from the truck. The thumping bass scared the hell out of Allen.

"Fuck the State Penn fuck hoe's in Penn State" (A line from Rapper Notorious B.IG).

Allen looked at the driver and shook his head. Before he knew, it the driver had gotten out of the SUV and walked up to Allen's car. Allen wanted to speed off and run the red light but he was at a major intersection. All Allen could think of was his wife and kids. He did not want to die while being robbed. The man knocked on Allen's driver side window. Allen rolled down his window, handing the man his wallet, his Rolex watch and car keys.

"I do not want any trouble, I have a wife and kids. Just take this," pleaded Allen.
The man laughed.

"Man you white cats are a trip. I got enough money to buy your car and your house. I was going to ask you if you had a jack. I just hit a pot hole and blew my tire out," said the man. Allen felt like a complete asshole.

"I'm sorry uh." "Save it man. It's not the first and it certainly won't be the last. I'm used to it by now.

"Wait, aren't you--" Before Allen could get his words out the man replied, "Yeah, I'm Mike Williams I play pro football.

"You're my son's favorite NFL Player." Just before the man got back in his truck he said.

"Hopefully your son will not grow up to be a racist asshole like his father."

The man flagged down others for help as they passed by. Allen drove home trying to forget what had just happened. He put it out of his mind quickly. Typical coon, he thought to himself. Allen's father Allen Sr. raised Langston and Allen, his only two sons, in the racist way of the South. Allen's mother Susan Thomas was the same way. Allen and Langston were taught that all people other than the white race were inferior to them. Allen senior, who had grown up in the deep backwoods of Mississippi, was a Grand Wizard in the Ku Klux Klan, and had moved to Virginia when he was a young boy. Although they moved north a little, that did not stop his family from maintaining their racist ways. Allen's father had passed away several years ago, but his views about race still flowed strongly through Allen's veins. Allen decided to swing by Stonewall Jackson Elementary to pick his son up early, after finding a place to park, Allen went to the office to pick up is son. James arrived shortly with his teacher, Ms. Lewis.

"Hello Sir, I'm Ms. Lewis. And you are?" said the young lady with her hand out.

She was African American. Allen gave a quick head nod instead of shaking her hand. She looked at him strangely.

"James had a good day today, but I am concerned about the pictures he drew today." The young lady showed Allen Sr. his son's drawings.

" It looks like a slave owner beating a slave with some type of pole or garden tool. And here you can see other slaves watching in the fields. I asked your son about this picture and he told me he was there when it happened and he even drew himself standing here." She said pointing to James in the picture. Allen was puzzled. "Sir I am concerned about this. Did you recently watch a movie? Maybe *Roots* or *Armistead?*"

"Uh yeah, we did. I'm sorry about that--you know how kids are." said Allen. "Yes, this is not uncommon. I figured he must have watched a movie that he remembered or had a dream about. Other than that, he is one of my best students," she said.

"Ok James see you tomorrow. Have a great day guys." Allen gave another head nod then walked out with his son. On the way home he questioned his son.

"What's going on?" "Why are you drawing these pictures?" James did not say a word he just stared at his father.

Allen did not want to tell his wife; she worried about everything. Allen balled up the picture and threw it out the window, but the picture flew right back in through the passenger window. Allen tried two more times to throw away the picture but it simply flew right back in the car. Allen then placed the picture on the back seat.

"You better not draw any more of this crap. Do you want to get kicked out of school?"

James shook his head left to right two quick times. The two pulled up to the house.

"Go to your room, James. I'll see you at dinner," said his father. Allen sat in the living room dumbfounded.

Maybe his negative ways about blacks were rubbing off too much on his son, although he was glad in a way, but he did not want him to be kicked out of school. Allen, unlike his late father, was not a smack in the face racist. He mostly kept his comments about other races, and his bigoted ways, in house and to himself. James sat in his room looking out the window, wishing Estella would come so his family would believe him. Tears ran down his face. As he looked out the window he could not believe how it looked as if nothing ever happened. There was no sign of people working or Estella.

Hours passed by. Soon the whole family was home. Allen told everyone that James had said a bad word and that was the reason he was in his room. Jenny and her mother went back out an hour after they arrived home, to the store for rice for dinner. Kevin was in his room getting his notebook in order for his classes. He had not spoken to his sister since their heated conversation. Suddenly his father walked in.

"What's going on?' said his father.

"Nothing much, first day at school and I have piles of homework." "Hey it's your senior year what do you expect," said his dad.

"Yeah. Hey, I was thinking about trying out for the basketball team." His dad laughed.

"What's so funny?" asked Kevin

"You kill me Kevin first it's this hip hop thing I'm trying to deal with, now you want to be a NBA star. It's an all-black league for crying out loud there is no room for skinny average height white boys. And those blacks can jump out the damn gym. I played college ball at Princeton before going for my masters at NYU, but I knew I was not cut out for the pros. We use our mind to get ahead while blacks use athletics," said Allen.

"Who said I wanted to go to the NBA? I thought you would support me on this." said Kevin.

"I will, son, but be realistic. What about soccer or tennis? I even heard your school has a great golf team. I was a good golfer in my day." Kevin turned from his dad and put on his headphones. Allen walked away still laughing to himself.

Three hours had passed since James was sent to his room. Allen went in to check on his son and found James asleep at the chair by the window.

"Hey there," said Allen. James awoke at his father's voice.

"Are you ready to come out of the room," asked his father.

"Yes," replied James.

"I told everyone you were in here for saying a bad word, ok? No more bad pictures, ok. Now most blacks are very bad people. There are a few good ones. You know like Oprah, Michael Jordan, and Colin Powell. But there's not many. Everyone does not think like us son. You cannot always say how you feel about them, ok?"

James was confused but nodded his head as if he did understand just to get out of the room.

"Come on, let's go downstairs."

"Can I play out front?" said James.

"Sure. Change out of your school clothes first, ok?"

James changed fast then headed outside. He really wanted to see if there was any sign of Estella. Once outside he looked all over, even venturing into the woods, but before he got any further his father yelled at him telling him not to go that far out. James went back

41

towards the house. He noticed his mother and sister pulling up. He ran to greet them with a hug.

"Hey James," said his mother.

"Bad day in school? No more bad words." said his mom.

"No more," agreed James. His sister gave him a kiss and they headed in.

James continued to walk around the house looking for his new friend. After an hour of looking he was called in to eat dinner. At the dinner table, everyone talked of how their day went, and how they felt about the new town and home. James listened but did not have anything to say; he simply ate his food and sat listening to everyone's conversation. He was relieved when it was time to leave the table. After he got up he approached his mother as she washed the dishes--it was an old-fashioned home with no dishwasher.

"Mommy, can I go back outside?" he asked in a timid voice, knowing it was getting dark out.

"It's a little dark; why don't you do some reading in your room. You have a book report due soon, don't you?"

He turned away and walked up to his room.

"Kevin, go read with your brother and make him feel better." said Tiffany to her oldest son.

"I have reading to do myself, I don't have the time." Kevin then dashed up to his room. Jenny was busy too.

Tiffany decided to read to James herself after she straightened up the house, but she was called in to the hospital. As a doctor she was almost always on call. James was left to read to himself. His father was also tied up with work. James read his book, and then played with his cars. Soon thoughts of the other world he entered with Estella entered his little mind. As time passed, he fell asleep in his bed.

Tiffany came in at nine forty-five, hoping he was up. As she entered the house, she dashed up to his room, but he was asleep with toys scattered all over the bed. Tiffany changed his clothes then tucked him in. Although he was asleep she whispered to him, promising him she would read to him the next day. She felt bad but in her line of work being away often came with the job. Tiffany showered up then headed to Allen's office. Allen was at work reading over cases his law firm was handling.

"Honey, it's getting late," she said, massaging his shoulders.

"Yeah, I know, I have about two or three more cases to review, and I will be to bed." She kissed her husband then headed to bed.

Kevin was on the phone with his best friend Derrick, telling him about the new environment. Jenny was asleep in the room. Within an hour, the Thomas family went to bed for the night. It did not take long for James to be awoken by taps on his window. James went to the window and saw Estella, who had been throwing pebbles at the window to wake him up. James opened the window.

"Can I come up," she yelled. James waved his hand signaling her to come up, and looking out, James saw all the people working again. This time, he knew he was not dreaming. He sat on his bed waiting for his friend. Slowly his door opened. Estella entered the room quietly.

"Hello, how are you?" said Estella.

"I'm ok. It's just that no one believes me when I tell them about you." said James.

"No one believes me either. Well, I think it's because you're so nice. And no white man is nice around here."

"Why do you say that?" said James.

"You do not understand yet, but you will after I show you. Come with me outside, and you will see," said the little girl, holding her hand out for James to grab. The two young children headed outside.

James noticed as he went down the stairs that the house was completely different. There were paintings along the walls. The men in the paintings were dressed as if they were in his history books. At the bottom of the stairs before going outside, James pulled away from Estella.

"What's wrong?" she asked.

"The house--it's not the same." The entire downstairs was changed. James was stunned and could not believe his eyes. Estella headed to the door and James followed her, entering Estella's world: a world that was far different than the one he lived in.

Estella knew that James really did not understand her world but she made it her mission to make sure James knew about the horrific, and egregious life of slavery. She worked in the Tabaco field's most of the time with her mother, Mabel. She always wondered off from work. Her mother said that she would be lynched one day if she kept abandoning her work, but Stella was a rebel like her late father.

Her Father was an enslaved man named Christopher Thomas, who was originally from Richmond. After his wife and two kids were sold to another plantation in Georgia, Christopher was traded to the Thomas plantation in Spotsylvania for a horse and 25 dollars. There he met Mabel and started a new family. They had four children; two were sold off to different plantations. Mabel never got over losing their two children, but sadly, Christopher was used to it. They never saw them again. Christopher made several attempts to run away. His plan was to run away then come back with help to get his family free. He hated slavery, and therefore was seen as a threat to Master Thomas. Christopher did not respect his master at all. He had been whipped several times, but it seemed he could not be broken. He attacked Master Thomas one day while working in the hot sun.

"Boy, you have been all damn day plowing this same area, and I see no results. You're a useless animal."

Christopher tried to block his master from his mind. Suddenly a lash from his master's whip came across his back. Christopher reacted like a lion that had cornered his prey for the kill. He knocked his master off the horse and punched him several times in the face, and then he began to choke him. He almost strangled his master to death, before two overseers came to Master Thomas' aid. He was lynched hours later. Estella was only two months old at the time, so she had no memory of her father. Many slaves spoke of Christopher and looked upon him as a legend. Estella had her father's blood pumping strongly in her veins. She had been whipped several times for talking back, leaving work unfinished, and stealing food from the big house. She often questioned her mother. Estella could not understand why they were treated so differently. Most slaves were too afraid to ask such questions, and simply accepted their way of life, but not Estella. She was a brave young girl.

James stood in the field with Estella.

"OK now, you see all these people working their called niggers," she said. "My Teacher said that's a bad word," said James.

45

"You're the first to say that. Every white man calls us niggers. That's all I know, but once a nice white lady that I cooked for said that we are black people. Anyway, just listen." said Estella with a laugh.

"We work from sunup to sundown. And we hardly get anything to eat. I often get whipped for stealing food, but Master Thomas's old lady Ellen, she gives me good food sometimes when no one is around. She is not as mean as master. She even taught me how to read a little when she could. My mom still says never trust any of them. I love reading. My grandmother always told me to learn one day, because she only knew but so many words. Sometimes I think it's useless to know how to read. If any slave finds out they will be jealous and they will tell Master. And a slave would be killed if Master found out they knew how to read. Master Thomas is a bad man." said Estella.

"Hey wait, my last name is Thomas."

"Maybe you are some kin to the master," she replied. James thought for a second; maybe he was. Estella knew he was but felt he would figure things out soon enough. "Come with me, I want to show you something." said Estella.

"Estella, you need to get back to work girl just 'cause Master is in town for the day don't mean you ain't working," said Mabel.

"Yes Ma, I'll be there."

Whenever Master went to town it was usually to buy more slaves or to get more tools for the field hands. Estella hardly worked at all when master left. Master Thomas's brother Billy kept watch over the slaves while he was gone. Estella took James to what the slaves called the bad tree. The bad tree was in the woods, about 200 yards from the field. Estella made James close his eyes as she led him to the bad tree. They soon were standing in front of the tree, and she told James to open his eyes. James was horrified and screamed at the top of his lungs. There on the tree hung a man, a woman, and a little girl.

"Calm down, boy. I'm a girl and you do not hear me screaming," said Estella who was already immune to the egregious treatment of slaves.

"Why did you take me here to see this?" said James.

"I wanted you to see how bad it is here. This was a family. The man is David, and that was his wife Ann and their daughter Beth. The Master raped Ann in front of David.

David hit the Master with a barrel. Then Master and his brother Billy and some other white man beat David badly. Then they hung his wife and daughter in front of him. Lastly they hung David and shot him. Master made all of us watch it from beginning to end. I cried for days; Beth was my best friend. After Master lynched them he set them on fire. Then he said if any of us ever strike him he would do the same to us."

James could not believe that a person could be so mean. "I have something else to show you. Come, follow me." Estella led the way. The two children walked about fifty yards or so. They approached a great crater in the ground.

"Look, there is where master puts the bodies of the slaves that disobey him." James looked upon a massive grave filled with human bones. James stepped back.

"I think I have seen enough," he said.

"No, I will show you much more of what goes on here, but not today. I have to get back to work; Master will be back soon. Hey, do you want to race back?"

Before Estella finished, James was already running. She quickly caught up to him and passed him, running straight into the field without realizing that Overseer Bill was standing in front of her. She tried to stop but she ran into Bill's leg.

"Nigger are you crazy?!" he said.

"I'm sorry, sir." Before she could finish, Bill struck her in the face, with a clenched fist knocking a tooth out. She lay unconscious on the ground. Bill began to kick her.

James ran up to stop him but he ran right through him as if he was a ghost. Tears ran down James's face. Bill would have killed Estella if it were not for Master's wife Ellen.

"Are you crazy, Bill?" she said, smacking him in the face. "This is a nigger, yes, but she is still a young lady." Bill stepped back and shook his head. In his mind, he thought, what a nigger lover.

"Go back to work," he yelled to all the slaves that had gathered around, including Mabel.

Mabel felt in her heart that her daughter would end up just like her late husband soon enough. Mabel picked Estella up and took her into the house to clean her up. The slaves where thankful that Ellen was not as coldhearted as every other white person they knew, but still they did not trust her. James sat on the grass crying. He could not believe what he had just witnessed. He got up and followed Mabel and Estella into a rundown shed. The shed was small with a dirt and grass floor. Mabel laid her daughter on a table. James wondered why there were no beds in the small room. He sat in the corner as Mabel tended to her daughter.

"It will be ok baby, it was a bottom tooth. It will not grow back you still mama's angel. Keep this cloth on your mouth. I have to get back to work. I will ask Miss Ellen if I can finish your part of work so you can stop working for the day. I will be back in a minute." Mabel left.

Estella was still in a daze. James walked up to her, touching her hand.

"Are you ok?" asked James." She looked at him and smiled. "I have been hit harder than this before."

"I think I have seen enough for today. I do not like this place. Why do they treat you like this?" said James.

"This is just how it is. My mama said it's always been like this for many years, but she did speak of a time when us black folks lived in a place called Africc Uh."

"Africa," said James.

"Yes, that's the place. My mom said black folks live freely there. She even said they are still living free there. Some of us run away to the north where blacks are free, but it's hard to run away."

"I wish you could live with me; it's not like that in my world. My teacher is black. Black people are free in my world," said James.

"Wow I cannot imagine it being any different than this. I would love to live in your world, but what about my mom? And I have brothers and sisters that are scattered all on different plantations. I cannot leave my family. Then there are all the other slaves." There was a long pause. James hugged Estella with tears in his eyes.

"You should go home now; your mom and dad may be looking for you," said Estella.

"OK, I will think of a way to free you," said the little boy.

James ran as fast as he could back to the house. The mean man that hit Estella was on the porch. James walked by him. He closed his eyes as he pushed open the door. When he walked in his eyes were still closed. He opened them to see his home intact as it normally looked, and then sighed in relief. James ran back up to his room and jumped in his bed. Although he was very much frightened, James soon fell fast asleep.

Estella knew she was a ghost and that the two worlds could not coexist. She only visited people whose hearts are pure. She lived as a slave until the age of 10 when she was lynched for trying to poison Master Thomas. She reenacted her life in a physical form; although it was painful to her to go back in time and relive harsh beatings and the ways of slavery, she felt it was the right thing to do if it would change someone's mind from prejudice.

Chapter 6

The next morning, the family was downstairs eating breakfast. Everyone was at the table except James. His mother went upstairs to get him, figuring that he might still be getting dressed for school. She went in the room to find her son still fast asleep.

"James, wake up," She said as she shook him.

"You are running late for school. Get up and hurry in the shower. I will have to drop you off; you will most likely miss the bus if you do not hurry."

James jumped up and got himself together quickly. After getting dressed he almost forgot to look out the window. He knew he would not see any sign of Estella, but he looked anyway. The many acres of land were like a ghost town. He shook his head as his mother called him downstairs. In his mind, he hoped Estella was okay. As the family headed out for the day, no one knew of the other world that James entered at night. He wanted to tell about it, but it was meaningless. He was a kid; no one would believe him.

Allen had a big meeting at work, but he stopped on the way to get an oil change. After that, he headed off to work. He had an all-white staff. He was glad of that. He did not have to worry about another situation like the one that happened with Todd back in New York.

His day went rather well. He even finished up early, leaving work around 1:15. He decided to go to the local gym where he had gotten a membership. When he got there he ran on the treadmill for about twenty minutes or so, and then went over to the basketball courts.

He was the only one in the gym. He shot around for about ten minutes. The suddenly he heard, "Yeah nigga I told you there would not be no one in here." Allen turned around. Several young black men entered the gym. They all headed down to the other court. There were nine of them. Allen did not want to play a full court game, knowing he would be the only white guy. He had played high school ball and two years of college ball.

He gave it up even though his coach told him if he worked hard he could have a shot at the pros. Allen's father always viewed the sport as a black sport. Allen quit the team in his third year.

He began doing the Micah drill.

"Hey old man, you trying to ball? "We need one," said one of the young men. "Uh, I'm ok, just shooting around."

"Man, people kill me coming in the gym, and don't want to run ball," said the young man.

"Man, that white boy cannot play anyway," added another. Allen was getting mad. He swallowed his pride and decided to play.

"Okay, I'll play," he said. He headed down the court. The shortest guy on the court was Allen, and he was six three.

The young men were tall and strong. The first play of the game, Allen was guarding one of the young men. The young man quickly dribbled past Allen and did a windmill slam-dunk. The kid must have jumped from the dotted line. Allen was amazed. He finally got the ball mid-way through the game. He hit four three-point shots.

"Not bad, old man," said one kid. After about ten minutes of running up and down the court, Allen was so out of shape, he felt as though he was going to pass out. He could not wait for the game to be over. The other team ended up winning the game. Allen knew he was the bad link in the chain for his team. The younger guys were far too quick for him.

"Good game, old man," said one of the young men holding his hand out. Allen gave a head nod and headed out the gym.

"What, you too good to shake my hand, man?"

"Your game was weak anyway," yelled the young man.

Allen left the gym and headed home. His body felt beat up. When he got home he soaked in the tub for an hour or so. He then laid down to rest his aching body.

Kevin waited outside of Robert E. Lee High Academy for his sister Jenny. Kevin was glad his dad let him drive the Beemer again. Everyone that walked by Kevin as he sat in the car looked at him strangely. It did not dawn on him at first that he was blasting "Reasonable Doubt," (a song from the rapper Jay-Z). Jenny walked to the car.

"Turn that mess off, you're embarrassing me," said Jenny.

"Whatever, when you get a car you can play what you want," said her brother while turning the music up a level higher.

The two kids drove off. A block up from the school Kevin noticed Daesha walking along the road.

"Hey, where are you going, need a ride?" said Kevin.

"I'm just going to the store up the road then walking back to school I have track practice in 30 minutes," said Daesha.

"I'll give you a ride. Better yet, we live 5 minutes up the road; I'll drop off my sister and take you to the store and practice." Daesha felt a good vibe with Kevin so she jumped in the car.

"I never rode in a BMW before; this is nice," she said. "Just a car," replied Kevin. As the two chatted, Jenny was pissed as they rode home. Kevin dropped his sister off and gave her a look that meant not to say a word. She went to the living room to watch T.V. Tiffany walked in with James, ten minutes later.

"Go to your room, James, we will see you at dinner," she said to her son. "What happened, mom?" asked Jenny.

"Well, your little brother told all the students in his class about black slaves and how he talks with one particular little black slave girl. He's getting out of hand with these stories. And the bad thing about it is that his teacher has not even taught black history yet this year. I'm puzzled how he knows these things."

"Maybe he has watched a slavery movie on his own in the past; he did have a TV with cable when we were in NYC," said Jenny.

"I'm hoping you're right honey. Hey, run out with me to the grocery store real quick. I forgot to buy some green peppers for the spaghetti tonight."

Tiffany and her daughter left shortly thereafter, while James stayed in his room. Kevin came in after dropping off Daesha. He was very attracted to her. She was on his mind a lot lately. Kevin went up to his room. He noticed his little brother's door was open so he entered the room.

"What's going on little bro?" asked Kevin. James did not utter one word. "Well, you can start talking anytime now."

James looked back out the window. He was tired of people not believing him. He promised himself that he would never tell anyone else about Estella or the other slaves. When

Kevin realized that his brother was not going to talk, he shook his head and headed to his room. James remained at the window until he was called down for dinner.

While at the dinner table James did not have much to say, he listened as the family went on about their day.

"So son, how was your day?" said Allen Sr. James did not say a word.

"He's still telling those bad stories in class to his class mates." said Tiffany. "Son, I told you that it's ok to talk about black people here at home but not in school!" Enough said you're in your room for the rest of the week."

"But dad!" said James.

"But dad, nothing. Finish up your food and go to your room." Tears began to rise in James's eyes.

Kevin was pissed. He hated when his father made remarks about black people.

"Is there something you'd like to say, Kevin?" Kevin got up from the table and went to his room.

"You can stay in your room for a week too. This is my house; you don't like it, leave," yelled Allen.

"Honey, calm down." Allen got up from the table and headed outside. Tiffany took James up to his room to get him ready for school the next day.
Jenny was the only one at the table. She picked up her cell and called her friend Karen; she talked to her as she finished her dinner.

Allen decided to take a drive to cool off. He drove into town and ended up at the park. Allen got out the car and walked around the baseball diamond. He had not been to the park since he was a kid, and now he was forty-five years old. Allen looked over at the tennis courts. A chill ran through his body. He had not been this close to the tennis courts since he was about sixteen. He was about two hundred feet away. He tried to get enough confidence to walk over to the tennis courts. With every step his heart raced, and flashes of what had happened at those courts went through his mind. He soon approached about ten feet or so from the court. In an instant Allen remembered everything that he had tried to forget. Then the terrible event flashed before his eyes.

There stood Allen and his girlfriend Melissa. They always walked through the park on their way home from school. Allen would get off at her stop just to walk her home. Melissa was beautiful. She had long red hair that turned a bronze color when the sun hit it just right and her eyes were like a deep blue sea. Allen often got lost looking into them. Melissa was so beautiful; she could have been a model. Allen loved to run his fingers through her wavy hair. The two would go to the tennis courts every day after school and kiss for hours.

"The sun is setting just right, Allen." said Melissa.

"It sure is."

"Allen, I really like you and I want to tell you something. I…" she paused shyly.

"What--say it?" pleaded Allen.

"I love you, Allen."

Allen's heart raced. He had loved Melissa ever since he first laid eyes on her.

"I love you too. I want to marry you one day, and have kids and a big house."

"Calm down," she said with a laugh,

"Let's take it slow," as she kissed Allen. Their moment was brought to an end quickly.

"Big payback. It's the big payback. I'm a man. I'm a son of a man (*a song by James brown*)." yelled four young black men walking towards Allen and Melissa, as they sang the famous James Brown song.

"Hey white girl. I know that white boy ain't hitting it right." said one of the young men. Allen and Melissa stood up from the grass. The young man grabbed Melissa's arm and she quickly snatched it away.

"Look guys, we do not want any trouble.

" Fuck you, white boy, you crackers got everything. We cannot even shit in a clean bathroom cause of you crackers."

"I know I'm not like that, I'm not for Jim Crow laws," said Allen, who at the time had not fully conformed to his father's racist propaganda.

Before Allen could finish his sentence, he was grabbed in a chokehold from behind. One of the young men grabbed Melissa as she screamed at the top of her lungs and Allen watched helplessly. The young man ripped her clothes from her until she was completely nude.

"If you keep screaming, I'll slit your throat bitch."

The young men had their way with Melissa. She looked at Allen with tears in her eyes as she was raped and forced to perform oral sex. After the three young men finished one grabbed Allen so the fourth young man could have his way with Melissa. Allen tried to break free. He bit the young man. Allen was then beaten until he lay unconscious, and left

to die on the tennis courts. As Allen lay unconscious, the men finished with Melissa then beat her to death and threw her body in the lake nearby. A young boy awaked Allen hours later with his father and their dog.

"Have you seen a girl? She was kind of tall with red hair," Allen said to the young boy.

"No, we have not, but you need to get to a hospital." The young boy and his father took Allen to the hospital.

Soon Allen's parents arrived. He told them the horrible story. Allen's father told him that the police were in search of Melissa and the four men. Later that next week while his parents were at his hospital bedside, Allen was told that Melissa's body was found floating in the lake. Allen screamed; his father and mother tried to calm him down as he tried to get out of the hospital bed.

Allen snapped back into reality and screamed suddenly, then realized he was on the tennis courts by himself. The middle aged man stood up with tears in his eyes. Allen's views of black people were never the same after the brutal rape and murder of his first love. His dad was just as he was with his kids. And Allen was like his son Kevin. He was not a racist from the start. Many of his father's views were on blacks were molding him somewhat, but since the day on the tennis courts he became a full-fledged racist, and he told himself he would never look at a black person the same. Allen strolled back to the car. He often thought of Melissa when he drove past those tennis courts. He would always quickly look away, but for some reason he did not on this day. Allen drove home, wishing he had not even stopped by the park.

Chapter 7

James tossed and turned all night. His friend Estella usually would have come to see him by now. Hours had passed. Every now and then throughout the night, James would go to the window, only to be disappointed. Just as sleep started to take hold of the little boy, he heard a tap at his window. James jumped out of the bed and ran for the window. It was Estella. She signaled for James to come outside. By this time it was a normal sight to the young boy to see the slaves, sweating hard in the fields and working. The two children embraced each other.

"I missed you, Estella, I thought you were badly hurt."

"I have had worse beatings than that, I told you. Overseer Bill can't hurt me," said the little girl. She began to walk away.

"Come on, silly." James followed her. The two children went into a rundown shack.

"Welcome to my home," said Estella. James looked around in disbelief at the state of Estella's living conditions. His room was nearly three times the size of the home that Estella shared with her mother. Estella pulled out an old bucket that was used for a chair. She sat on it.

"I have shown you a lot of the way it is in my world. Everything you have seen was for a reason. I already know that no one believes you. As long as you know, you have to promise me you will not treat people this way, no matter what their color is," said Estella.

"I would never do these bad things. I wish I could say the same about my dad," said James sadly. Estella peeped out of the broken door of her shack.

"I better get back to work soon. I can read your heart. I know I said I would show you more, but our time is done. You are the only person in that house that was not afraid. Over the years, I have been trying to find someone that would listen to my story. Well, not just my story, but the story of my people."

"I wish my dad could see this--how wrong your people have been treated." The two children paused in silence."

"I got it; maybe I will come to him. Better yet, my grandpa Larry will come visit your father. He knows of the beginning, before America when we black people was free in Africa. I will get him to meet your father."

"Yes, then he will believe me," said James.

"And hopefully change his ways," added Estella. "Now go home, I must get back to work. We will meet again. But our time is done now. Do not forget me."

"I will never forget you," said the little boy as a tear fell from his face. The two children hugged, and then Estella went back out to work. James walked back to his house. He looked at Estella working hard next to her mother in the blazing sun. Just as he got to the steps to open the door,

"What the hell are you doing boy," yelled his father.

"Look, I told you dad, look at the people in the field working." It seemed in a split second it was pitch-black dark outside.

"Boy, it's two in the morning. Get your butt in the bed now!" said Allen as he slapped James on the behind. Allen shut and locked the door, then followed his son to the room. "Look, this game is over. If I hear another word about slaves at school here at home or wherever, I swear you will never see the daylight again; you'll be grounded for life," said Allen as he slammed the door. James quickly ran to the window. As he looked out the window, he could not believe how day turned into night so fast. How the people had disappeared. James jumped in the bed, hoping Estella would keep her word.

It was Saturday morning. The family slept in. James was the first one up, so he made himself some Pop Tarts in the toaster, and then sat by the window in his room, until he heard his mother wake up. James hoped that his father would not tell everyone what had

59

happened last night. James was worried that his father would be more watchful of him at night time now. This would mean that he could not sneak out to see Estella.

Allen decided to take the family to Washington D.C. for the day, out of the blue. Allen would surprise the family with a road trip every now and then. D.C. was only an hour or so away. The huge monuments astonished James. Although Allen was having fun spending time with his family, thoughts of what happened at the tennis courts ran rapidly throughout his mind, although he hid it well from everyone.

After an hour or so at the National Mall the Thomas family headed over to the Lincoln Memorial. Allen took pictures of the family in front of the monument.

"You know, Lincoln helped free the slaves, and Martin Luther King gave his "I have a Dream speech" here." said Kevin to his father. Allen looked at his son and then replied with a chuckle.

"That was only to save the union, he did not care about slavery." Kevin was not surprised in his father's response.

"Come on guys, it's been three hours today. Let's head home," said Tiffany. After grabbing a bite to eat the family jumped on 395-South to head back home.

It was late in the evening. James was fast asleep in the car. He was so sleepy that he did not even feel his mother changing his clothes and putting him in the bed later when they got in. The family stayed downstairs. Allen had rented a horror movie from the video store. He was trying to spend as much time with his family as possible, hoping it would free his mind of Melissa and the past. After the movie, it was about 1 am. Everyone headed up to bed.

Allen decided to finish looking over resumes, since he had planned to hire a new lawyer. He had received about thirty resumes and had them narrowed down to ten. He planned to go through them so he would have all of Sunday to relax. About an hour into work Allen fell asleep at his desk and in ten minutes, he was in a deep sleep.

He was awakened by an extremely cold draft. As Allen raised his head from the table he was startled. There in front of him stood a black man about six three or six four. The man was dressed as if he was very poor; his clothes were almost all torn rags. Allen was shaking. Then suddenly the man spoke.

"Sir, my name is Larry Thomas I come to pay you a visit," said the man in a very deep voice. Allen arose from his chair. His heart raced. Just as he stood, Larry covered his face as if Allen was going to strike him.

"I do not know who the hell you are but you'd better get the hell out of my house before I call the police."

Allen suddenly went to grab Larry's arm but instead he grabbed nothing but air. Allen then took two steps away from the man. Allen quickly realized that that the man was a ghost.

"Just come with me, sir," said the man. Allen, now in fear for his life, followed the man as he headed for the door.

As soon as the door opened, all Allen could see was the deck of a vast ship. The sun was shining so brightly that he had to cover his eyes. Allen looked back and his home was gone. There were men walking about the ship dressed in colonial-style clothes, similar to what Thomas Jefferson might have worn. Allen was shocked, pinching himself to see if he was dreaming and hoping he would wake up at his desk, but to no avail he was still on the ship. Allen followed the man as they walked towards the end of the ship. When they reached the end of the ship, Larry sat on a barrel, and then pulled one up for Allen to sit on. Allen sat and looked back to where they had walked from; hoping to see his house, but there was no house in sight.

61

"Look, I do not know what the hell is going on but I need to get back to my family," said Allen.

"I know, sir, but I came to you to teach you and show you a lesson in what my people have been through. Just watch and learn, sir."

From what Allen could tell, it was the early morning. The men on the boat were talking and smoking tobacco in their pipes. Seagulls flew over the ship. Allen looked around, still thinking that he was dreaming. He walked around the boat, realizing the men did not see him. He walked right up to one man in particular. The man was the captain of the ship; Capt. Jack Voit was his name. Jack had been making trips from Africa to America for about ten years. Allen waved his hand directly in the man's face, but he acted as though nothing had happened. Allen turned and looked at the great ocean. The sea was rough and he could see wave's miles away. There was no sign of land. Allen turned to walk back to the barrels, noticing that the old man that brought him there was no longer sitting on the barrels. Now he was alone, and scared. Allen could not make sense of what was happening, where he was, and why. Then suddenly he heard a man yell.

"Rise and shine niggers," yelled a man as he began to open up the floor of the ship. A man came up from the hold of the ship chained to another man; that man was chained to a woman; the woman chained to a young boy; and so on and so forth.

Within minutes the large ship was filled with African slaves. Allen could not believe his eyes, realizing that he had gone back in time somehow. He watched as the slaves stood in lines on the boat. All of the slaves looked young; the oldest that Allen noticed had to have been no older than twenty-six or so. He watched as the captain examined the slaves.

"You niggers sure do smell. I think it's time for a salt-water bath. Several men on the ship immediately began pouring buckets of salt water on the slaves. Some slaves screamed, and others did not budge. Suddenly, a young slave girl passed out on the deck.

"Capt. Jack this nigger bitch is very sick, sir. She passes out every time we bathe them. And every time we feed her she refuses to eat."

"I have the solution to that." said Jack.

Allen watched as Capt. Jack walked over to the young girl. He picked her up and tossed her overboard. Allen could not believe what he had just witnessed.

The girl was probably his daughter Jenny's age. Allen ran over to look over the boat. He saw the young girl screaming for her life as the sea soon swallowed her. Right after the Capt. Jack drowned the young girl another female started screaming. Allen figured that she must have been close to or related to the young girl. Capt. Jack punched the girl in the face as if she was a man. The girl dropped to the deck, bringing down the man beside her due to them being chained together.

"Stupid nigger bitch I should toss you over too. Better yet, take her to my room and clean her up, then put her in my bed to keep it warm till I get back there in a few," he said with a laugh. Capt. Jack was heartless, Allen thought.

Capt. Jack demonstrated running in place. Then he made the slave do so.

"Captain," said one man. "We have lost twenty one niggers already. We cannot afford to lose any more, sir."

"Mark, calm down; we reach the shores of the Chesapeake in two days. We have more than enough slaves. There's no need to fear. You and all the other men will earn thirty dollars and your choice of a young buck or a nigger bitch for free," said Capt. Jack.

After thirty minutes of exercise, the slaves were ordered back down into the ship's belly. Allen sat on the barrel and watched the men fish off the side of the ship. He missed his family and wondered if he would ever see them again. He wondered if this was his punishment by God for treating blacks so wrong throughout his life. Allen soon fell asleep on the barrel after watching the waves for an hour. He hoped he would wake up from a bad dream.

Chapter 8

Tiffany noticed that when she went down to cook breakfast, the front door was wide open. She searched outside and in the back of the house for her husband.

"Allen," she yelled several times at top of her lungs. She went in to search the house. It was so strange. She would always find him asleep in his office if he stayed up late working. She told the children.

"Maybe Dad went in to the office in town," said Jenny.

"You're right," said her mother. Tiffany called his office, but there was no answer.

She jumped in the car and drove by the office, but the doors were locked and all the lights were off. She drove back to the house trying to think positively about the situation. When she got home Jenny had made breakfast. The family tried to carry on with the day as they always would have. Tiffany sat in the living room staring out of the window. James approached her.

"Daddy will be okay, Mommy, he's fine."

"Thanks, son," said Tiffany as she kissed him on the forehead. She wanted to believe her son.

"Yeah, Dad's fine. It's not like we have a high crime rate here. He's probably out golfing with the boys," said Kevin. All her children's assumptions made her worry more for some reason. James knew exactly where his dad was. He knew Estella had not let him down, but he did not want to tell his family because he knew they would not believe him.

By nightfall Tiffany was worried sick. She had called the police and told them her husband was missing. Of course, they told her there could be no missing person's report filed for 24 hours, but that they would investigate. She could not sleep that night, so went in her daughter's room and the two women lay in bed, fearing they would never see Allen again. As James lay in bed, he wondered when his father would return. Soon James was

asleep.

Jenny's friend Teresa picked her up for school the next morning. Teresa consoled Jenny, who was now a complete mess was worrying about her father. Kevin, on the other hand, was not too worried. There even was some relief not to have his stern racist dad at home. He figured his mom and dad had a fight, and his father may have gone back to NYC to cool off for some time. His dad had done so in the past. Kevin had a woman on his mind. He had gotten Daesha's number the day he dropped her off at practice, but he had not called her yet. He finally got the nerve that morning. He called her on his cell as he drove to school. As the phone rang, thoughts of his dad's mysterious disappearance ran through his head. He was in denial that his dad's disappearance was serious, but at the same time, he needed someone to talk to. Those thoughts were shattered instantly by Daesha's sweet voice.

" Hello." "Yeah, uh, hey, it's me. Kevin. Just headed out to school and wondered if I could pick you up?"

"Okay, um, I'm just finishing my hair. Meet me at that store you dropped me off at the other day; it's walking distance from my house."

"Okay, see you soon." Kevin hung up, having felt butterflies in his stomach throughout the conversation. Daesha actually lived twenty minutes or so from that store, so she got her mom to drop her off.

"So baby, you met a young man. I can't wait to meet him. Is he dark, brown, light skin?" said Loraine as she drove her daughter to the store. Daesha looked out the window as the road in the car.

"He is light skinned Mom, um, you can let me out right here."

"Okay, if you say, so but the store is a little way up," said her mom.

"I'm good." She kissed her mother and headed up the road to the store to meet Kevin.

She knew in her heart her mother would have a fit if she told her Kevin was white, but she figured she would cross that road if she and Kevin got serious. Kevin pulled up as she was about ten feet away from the store. He got out of the car and opened her door.

"Okay mister, you get points for that one," said Daesha. Kevin smiled. The two headed off to school.

Throughout the week they spent more and more time together. That Saturday night they went to the movies. They conversed as the coming attractions came on before the movie started.

"So how are you taking your dad's disappearance; I am sure it's rough?"

"I mean, I miss him, but not his ways. I feel comfortable around you now, so I will be real with you. My dad is a racist. He hates blacks and pretty much any other race that is not white." Daesha could not believe her ears.

"Are you serious?"

"Yes, and so is my mother and sister. But I'm not like that at all, as you can tell. I

66

don't look at race I look at the person. My father hated the fact that my best friend was black.

I believe he moved the family from Manhattan to this town to have less exposure to blacks.

Are you more comfortable if I say African American?"

"Boy, its ok. That's crazy because honestly, my mother is the same way. I mean,

she would trip out if she knew I was dating a white guy. I never considered myself even

attracted to white guys. They never looked my way."

"Daesha you're so beautiful a blind man would look your way." She smiled.

"You're so sweet. I thought you were a hottie when we met in the hallway that day."

The two looked into each other's eyes and then it happened: the first kiss. It was

amazing. Kevin asked her to be his girl later that night after the movie and she accepted.

They knew their relationship would be rough, but they were ready.

Chapter 9

Allen awoke, hoping to see that he was at home waking from a nightmare, but instead he found himself in the belly of the ship. He was chained together to a slave male. Allen tried several times to get out of the chains, but they would not budge. All he could hear was people's cries. There was barely any light. He could see there were people lying on the floor, all chained together. Some were throwing up. Others where urinating, and making bowel movements. The smell was overwhelming. Allen started to gag, wishing he could cover his nose and mouth but his hands were chained. The ship rocked back and forth. After two hours he began to be seasick. Now Allen had to throw up. He felt so sick.

Suddenly he heard a voice.

"How does it feel, Allen." It was Larry kneeling down beside him, the slave spirit who had taken Allen from his home.

"Please get me out of here; take me to my family," cried Allen. "In due time, Allen. I want you to feel the pain and the struggle."

This was only the beginning. Larry slowly disappeared. Allen screamed out but he had already vanished. The other slaves thought Allen was crazy for talking to himself. Days went by. Allen must have been in the belly of the ship for three or more days. Finally, the hatch was opened and the hot sun shined into the belly of the ship. The cries of the slaves were at their highest peak now. Allen also cried out for food and water. The slaves were brought out of the ship for food, water, and to bathe and exercise. Capt. Jack walked up and down the ship examining slaves. Soon, he stood over Allen as he ate the leftover slop that the Captain and his men did not finish.

"I don't think I have seen this nigger before." "Mark, get over here." said Capt. Jack. Mark quickly ran over to the Captain.

"Yes sir?" " Mark, have you seen this nigger before? I examine each and every slave, and I do not remember this one."

"All these monkeys look alike, I say sir," said Mark with a laugh.

"Yes, you're right." Allen stood up.

"I'm not a slave. I'm white, can't you see. Get me out of these chains and these rags for clothes." What Allen heard himself say was plain English, but to Capt. Jack It sounded like an African language he did not know. Capt. Jack punched Allen in the face.

"Shut up nigger when I'm examining you." Allen fell down. He jumped up and tried to fight back, but before he could throw a blow, Mark hit him in the back of his head with a barrel knocking him out cold.

Capt. Jack unchained him from the slave he had been linked to, and dragged his body.

"Thanks, Mark I have no time for young bucks with no respect. Help me throw this animal overboard."

The two men grabbed Allen and put half of his body over the ship. Allen awoke and all he could see was the ocean. He looked up and saw two men holding his legs. Allen screamed for his life.

"Sir, are you sure you want to do this? He is a healthy, young strong buck. And one of the biggest niggers we have." said Mark. Capt. Jack paused for a second.

"Maybe you're right. He may make good money, and a good field hand if broken the right way."

The two men pulled Allen back down on to the ship. Capt. Jack ordered Mark to whip Allen. Allen was taken into the ship and made to walk down a long hallway. He noticed several doors and glanced in one room as he walked by. He saw a young slave girl, about

69

twelve or so. She was screaming as one of the men from the crew raped her. Allen shook his head.

"What are you looking at nigger?" yelled the man. Allen quickly looked to the ground. Allen was led into the torture room, a room used to break slaves when they were out of line.

Allen noticed bloodstains all over the walls. He even saw some teeth on the ground. Allen was stripped naked and chained with his face to the wall. His fists clenched in fear of what the first lashing would feel like.

"Time to break a nigger," yelled Mark in a loud voice.

Five men from the crew came in after hearing the first lashing. Allen screamed at the top of his lungs. The pain was unbearable. The louder Allen cried, the louder the men laughed and the harder the men swung the whips. He was hit twenty times, but by the fourth lash he had passed out. All the slaves in the hold of the ship could hear Allen's screams.

He was dragged back out, unconscious, and chained back to the bottom with the other slaves. When Allen finally woke up a day later, he was being pulled back on the deck of the ship with the other slaves. All of them were lined up on the ship, which was a day out to come to the shore. All the slaves were stripped, including Allen. They were bathed with soap and warm water.

"We must make them look good. It's time to cash in men. The auction is taking place tomorrow. I want the niggers to look halfway decent," said Capt. Jack. The slaves were cleaned thoroughly, for the first time since they had been aboard the ship.

"Let the niggers stay on deck. The smell in the belly of the ship from these animals will defeat the purpose of bathing them," said Capt. Jack.

Allen felt weak. He told himself the next time he saw the spirit he would beg Larry to take him back to his family. The slaves danced on the ship and sang songs as the crew laughed at them. Allen was still in disbelief at the situation. He looked at his skin; he was filthy, but it was clear to him that he was white. Why didn't the crew see the same thing as he did? Allen stood up; the sun was shining hard on the beautiful ocean. Allen looked down at the water. He nearly passed out when he saw that he was black. He stood flummoxed as he looked at his reflection in the water. He even waved his hand and saw the same wave from the black man in the water. He was black. Allen sat in the corner. This must surely be hell. Allen began to pray for God to forgive him for everything wrong that he ever did to any race of people and to please allow him to be back with his family. Nightfall soon came; the slaves were relieved to sleep in the fresh air instead of in the hold. Allen tossed and turned on the hard oak wood floor. He could not sleep. Allen had no idea of the pure dehumanizing encounter that would happen the next day.

The slave ship had stopped at Jamestown Island. It was just daybreak as all the slaves were led off the ship. Most of them stumbled and fell when they took more than five steps. They had not walked any real distance in months. Some 580 slaves were aboard. The ship was only built to hold 450 slaves, but they were crammed into any crevice possible. Some were even packed on top of each other. This particular slave ship was in sections separating men, women, and children. Each deck in the hold had a section. This was how so many could be crammed in a compact space. After about twenty minutes, all the slaves were off the ship. The auction was only four or five miles away. The town had grown vastly since the start of the slave trade. After the five-mile walk Allen's feet were aching. He could understand all the words being said by Capt. Jack, but Allen still could not understand why they could not understand his words. Allen noticed a large crowd of people in front of a huge barn yard shaped doors. As the crowd rambled on loudly, Capt. Jack pulled out his pistol. He shot once in the air.

"All have gathered here in Jamestown for the purchase of slaves. First off, all our young good bucks will go for $50 dollars. Older slaves will go between $15 and $20 dollars. Once the nigger is mounted on stage, potential buyers may come and examine your chattel. Then Mr. Shifflet will begin bids. Let's get started."

As soon as Capt. Jack finished, the crowd went on talking loudly amongst one another. The majority of the men in the crowd were rich slave-owners who came from generations of slave owning. The slaves were brought into the auction doors five at a time. Allen was miserable. He wanted badly to be out of his chains. His wrists and ankles where bleeding on and off. Every time a scab would heal some overnight, they would re-open when he moved. What was even worse was that the other slaves could communicate among each other. He did not understand anything they were saying. After two hours of standing in a slow moving line Allen was now near the front and could see what was going on. A young slave woman stood on stage.

"This nigger bitch will be perfect for breeding. She is about sixteen or seventeen. I will start the bid." said Mr. Shifflet. Before he could yell out a starting price a man in the crowd yelled out.

"I take her for one hundred dollars," said the man. No one outbid him. "Sold!" said Mr. Shifflet.

"I still want to examine her," said the man as he stepped onstage. He handed 100 dollars to Mr. Shifflet and stood in front of the young girl, who trembled in fear. She had no idea what was going on. The man stripped her clothes off. There she stood naked in front of the crowd of men, women, and children. The man walked around her, looking at her buttocks. He fondled her repeatedly. Finally he took her away. Her two sisters were in line waiting to be sold. They screamed as their sister went away, never to be seen again.

Allen could not believe what he was witnessing. Slowly but surely, Allen's time came. He was placed on stage. Allen stood on stage and his mind went blank. He could not believe what was happening to him. Mr. Shifflet began his bids. Allen was so overwhelmed by what was happening that he passed out. When he regained consciousness, he was in the back of a wagon. He was still shackled both hands and feet.

"You finally up, nigger. You're a good-sized buck, and even though you passed out on me, I still bought your ass. Others thought you were too sick. I know money-making chattel when I see it. I know you will come in handy this Tabaco season." The voice came

from Mr. Carter.

Mr. Carter was just starting to gain political respect in his small town in Chancellorsville County, Virginia. He owned about thirty slaves. His plans were to also use Allen as a breeder. With Allen's size, he thought, he would make many strong male slaves. It was about a six hour ride from Jamestown back home. When Mr. Carter arrived, his wife was glad to see him.

"Hello, honey." said Wilma. "What did you buy?" Just as she said that Allen rose from the wagon. "My, my, he's a strong looking buck. What will we name him?" She asked her husband.

"Hell, he's the biggest nigger I ever seen. Let's just call him Buck."

Mr. Carter broke slaves he had, by beating them half to death and by raping the women. Mr. Carter even took pleasure in raping male slaves, especially the big ones. He believed by taking their manhood they would be in more fear and respect their master more.

73

Many slave owners used this method of breaking a male slave called, Breaking the Buck. They would beat the male slave so badly that they were too weak to fight off being raped. He tied Allen's feet to a tree branch. He let his wife beat Allen first then he finished him off. Allen screamed until the point where there was no more pain. It was just a lash tearing away flesh down to the bone. After the brutal beating, Mr. Carter laid Allen in a shed. Mr. Carter told his wife to head back to the house and make dinner. She had no idea that her husband raped male slaves. She knew of him raping the female slaves. That seemed to be a norm, and most wives of slave owners had learned to ignore it. Allen had no idea what was about to happen to him as he lay on the floor too weak to move. Mr.

Carter tied Allen's hands behind his back, and his ankles. Allen lay hogtied on the ground. Then Mr. Carter balled up a cloth and shoved it into Allen's mouth.

"You young big bucks have to learn the hard way." said Mr. Carter, as he unbuttoned his pants. He mounted Allen, choking him from behind as he sodomized him.

Allen screamed. He could not believe what was happening to him. When Mr. Carter was done, he left a crying Allen trembling on the floor.

Soon the morning came. Mr. Carter figured that his new slave was broken in. Mr. Carter went to the shed. There lay Allen clinging on to life. Mr. Carter untied Allen and then threw a bucket of salt water on him.

"Get up, Nigger." The salt water ate away at Allen's cuts and old scabs. Allen quickly jumped up, screaming.

"Why me? What did I do wrong," yelled Allen, but of course this was African gibberish to Mr. Carter. Allen was taken to the field, where he saw slaves working hard.

He was given a bag to pick Tabaco. As Allen looked into the vast field, the Tabaco fields seemed to stretch on infinitely. The sun was shining extremely hard. Allen was miserable.

"Now that bag better is to be filled to the top by tonight," then Mr. Carter showed Allen his slave quarters.

"That's the shed you will live in. Night will guide you and get you up to speed," said Mr. Carter as he walked away to check on his other slaves.

As Allen picked Tabaco, he wondered if he would ever see his family again.

"Feel the pain yet," said a voice. It was Larry. Allen dropped the bag of Tabaco and quickly grabbed the man's legs.

"Please, I beg you, take me home to my family. I have suffered long enough," cried Allen.

"Oh really? African Americans have suffered through hundreds of years of slavery.

Families torn apart, woman raped, slaves lynched. I can go on and on. And you have been a slave for two days now. And you feel you have suffered enough," said Larry.

"Please forgive me. I never meant to be racist against your people. I had my reasons," said Allen.

"I know about your past, but you cannot fault every colored person for it. You still have much learning to do," said the slave as he began to fade away. Allen pleaded for him to stay, but soon enough, he was gone.

There was Allen in the midst of a Tabaco field; the sun's rays were furious. Allen could not believe how the others worked as if the sun did not affect them. Allen began to feel he would never see his family again. He even wondered if he had really died and gone to hell.

Chapter 10

Tiffany sat in the living room in complete darkness. The kids were over at their Uncle Langston's house. Greg came up for the holidays; it was Thanksgiving Day. Tiffany had started smoking again. She had not smoked since she was seventeen, but after her husband's disappearance she had become a regular chain smoker. She was supposed to meet everyone at five, but it was now six fifteen. It seemed Tiffany cried every day. She loved Allen with all her heart. For him to just up and leave just did not seem right. She thought he was in love with her. As Tiffany smoked and cried to herself, there was a knock at the door. She wished it was her husband, as she did every time the phone rang, but this time she did not even bother to get up. The door opened and it was Christina.

"Tiffany, are you ok? I was making sure everything was fine. Girl, you're still in your robe," said Christina.

" I think I will stay here; just bring me a plate later," said Tiffany sadly.

"I will not take no for an answer. You have been out of work for almost two months now. Just moping around this house, sitting in the dark all the time," said Christina.

"What the fuck am I supposed to do? What if it was Langston that just up and left? No clue, no fucking trace. Then what? The father of my children and love of my life is gone, for crying out loud," yelled Tiffany with tears streaming down her face.

There was a pause between the two women. Christina hugged Tiffany.

"I'm so sorry, honey. Let's just have Thanksgiving. The family wants you there," said Christina.

Finally, after an hour of pleading, Tiffany got herself together and headed over with Christina. The two women walked across the gravel road. Kevin and Greg looked at them in the distance.

"Dude, I hope your mom will be ok. She is taking it the worst, I think." said Greg.

"Yeah, I mean, it's puzzling. Why would he just leave us? The crazy thing about it is that he did not take anything. He left all his clothes, the car, everything, man."

"Maybe he did not want any memories. He may have wanted to have a complete new start," said Greg.

"That's what I told mom, but she is convinced he will come back," said Kevin.

The Thanksgiving dinner was quiet for the most part. There were the usual requests to pass the salt or pass the gravy, but there was no real conversation. Finally, Langston broke the ice.

"So how is basketball season going, Kevin?"

"I did not make the team, remember?"

"Oh, I'm sorry." Langston figured he'd tried enough. The family kept eating in silence.

After dinner was over, Kevin and Greg went for a drive. Cristina drove Jenny, James, and their mother back home. As Greg and Kevin drove into town, Greg wanted to tell Kevin of his experience in the house, but he did not, and Kevin did not mention anything else strange about the house.

"Man, so are the Marines treating you right?" asked Kevin.

"I mean, it's a guaranteed paycheck, that's all I can say. I'm thinking about being an officer. It's better, I think."

"Man, I was thinking about joining. I see how chicks are all over you when you come home in those dress blues, man."

"Please don't join for the uniforms, man," said Greg with a laugh. "I hope your dad is ok man, not to change the subject."

"Me too. As much as I miss him, I hated him at times. It's weird some parts of me are glad he's gone."

"What the hell is wrong with you!" said Greg.

"You know as well as I do my dad was a flaming racist just like your father. He kept trying to make me, and the rest of the family that way my whole life. I'm not like that. I do love and miss my father, but now that he is gone I can breathe easy. I have met this black girl in town, and we have been talking for some time. I met her while my dad was here, but now that he's gone I feel free to really be myself."

"I understand where you're coming from; my dad is the same way. And I was a racist too at one point, but the Marine Corps has no color. When I was on a mission one night, my fire team was driving over a bridge when it collapsed into the Tigris River. I managed to get out of the Humvee. But I had on so much gear I was sinking to the bottom. I did not know that Staff Sergeant Stephen had already swum over to the bank, near the bridge. My fire team was being swept away by the currents of the river, and we were being fired at by insurgents. Staff Sergeant Stephen jumped in the river swam to me, and saved my life. He put me on his back and took me to safety away from enemy fire. And a month before that after he heard me say a racist joke, he asked me was I a racist and I told him yeah; we had not spoken again until the day he saved me. Now we are best friends, and I have changed. I guess what I'm saying is your father needs something to happen to him, something to change his views on other races."

"You're right Greg." "Who knows, maybe if you see him again he will be a changed man."

Jenny and her mother folded clothes in the laundry room. James sat on the floor playing with his toy trucks.

"Mom I'm taking the SATs next month. If I get and 1200 or more I can go to UCLA with my grades."

"That's good to hear," said Tiffany. Jenny was always trying to make her mother smile since her fathers disappearance, but it was useless; she had not smiled since her father's disappearance. Jenny kept folding clothes in silence. James decided to go up to his room to get more trucks to play with. When he opened his door he was startled. There was Estella sitting on his bed.

"Boy, I was wondering when you would come in." The two embraced one another.

"Where's my dad?" asked James.

"He is okay; he's learning like you did."

"Yes, but when I learned I came back home every night. My mommy misses my dad. And I do too."

"Be patient, James. He will return when the time is right. Do you want to see him?" asked Estella.

"Yes, can my mommy come?"

"No, only you."

The two walked down the stairs. Tiffany heard her son walking toward the door.

"James, if you're going to play with your trucks outside, stay close by; it's getting dark."

"Okay," yelled James. Tiffany heard him talking to someone but paid it no mind. When the two stepped out the door, instantly they were in the other world.

"This is another plantation. Master Carter owns this one. Your dad was brought here to learn of the horrific life of slavery."

The two walked the dirt road that had suddenly appeared when they left James's home. They climbed the fence into the field. James got stuck on the way over the fence, so Estella had to help him. Slaves were everywhere in the fields performing tasks like picking Tabaco, plowing, and painting the Big House. Allen was slaughtering pigs in the barn with another slave by the name of Night. Night was given his name for his very dark skin.

"Two more hogs to go. You think Master will cut us loose? He say he only want six; we done did eight," said Night.

"You never know with him." Said Allen.

Allen never discussed his past life with any other slave. He felt no one would believe him. He had accepted his new life. He was glad that Larry the slave spirit allowed him to communicate now with other slaves.

The two children approached the barn.

"There's your father, working hard," said Estella. James tried to run up to his dad but Estella grabbed his arm. "Remember he cannot hear or see you."

"But I want to talk to him."

"Not now, Allen," said Estella. A horse and carriage pulled up. It was Master Carter. He got out of the carriage with his mighty whip in hand. He walked right past the two children, and into the barn.

"You boys done yet?"

"Yes, sir," said Night. "We got eight hogs done, and you only wanted six, massa." Master Carter wanted a reason to show his authority.

"Nigger, I said ten hogs," said Master Carter.

"That you did, massa, I'm so sorry, sir." "Now you're a nigger, that's expected of you. You cannot count. You have the mind of the very pigs you slaughtered.." said Master Carter. Allen was furious and wanted badly to tell Master he was wrong.

"You want to say something Buck?" Master Carter struck Allen across the face with his whip. Allen hit the ground screaming. "Now finish these hogs up," said Master Carter as he walked off.

James broke away from Estella and ran to his father's side. He looked as his dad lay on the ground in pain. Estella came to his side.

"He will be okay, I promise. Let's go now." Before James could blink, he was back in front of his own house.

"Our work is almost done with your father. He will be a changed man, hopefully, when he returns. I promise," she said. James wiped his tears and went in the house.

"Is that you James," yelled Tiffany.

"Yes, Mommy."

"You did not hear me calling you twenty minutes ago? I sent your sister out to look for you. Go get washed up for bed."

James knew his dad would come home soon; he just wished his mom knew that. Kevin could not sleep. He wondered if he was too hard on his father, but then again maybe Greg would be right and his father, if he returned, would be a changed man. Parts of Kevin missed his dad, but sadly most of him didn't. Jenny was just as hurt as her mother. Her dad could do no wrong in her eyes. It was going on two months since their father had disappeared without a trace.

Tiffany was determined to get into a routine without Allen. Although thoughts often ran through her head that her husband might be dead, she would always put them out of her mind as quickly as they came. Hope and faith kept her going. She had never been more religious than since Allen's disappearance; Tiffany had been a regular at the Sunday services. She also prayed at least five to six times a day. She was determined not to give up hope. Throughout her day she would often say things to the children as if Allen was there. She even told Jenny to take Allen's favorite sports coat to the cleaners one day.

Allen lay in his small shack. The moon shone brightly into his small living quarters. Allen could not believe how inhumane African Americans were treated in slavery. He was indeed changing. He had a compassion that he never had before for people of another race besides his own. He had received several beatings since he came into the life of a slave. He had witness raping of women, and the lynching of slaves. He even witnessed a slave female set on fire for trying to run away. All this was taking a toll on Allen. Night mentioned to him earlier that day that he was planning to run away. Allen had it in his mind that he was not going to see his family again, so he thought he might as well try to make an escape. He had nothing to live for anymore. He had not seen the spirit who had brought him into slavery in weeks. He thought he would never see him again.

Maybe this was his new life. Allen wondered if maybe he had had a heart attack while working at his desk that evening and died, and now he was reincarnated as a slave. Allen's mind continued to ramble with crazy thoughts.

That morning Allen and Night had to chop up wood for the winter. Since they were the two biggest slaves on the plantation, chopping wood was their job. The two men often got the hardest jobs. They began chopping wood at five am. Master Carter did not give them a break that whole day; they worked until nine that night. All they received was left over slop for dinner. The two men ate their meal after a long day's work. They were sure they were done for the night. As they ate their food, Master Cater went to check on them.

"You boys worked hard today," said Master. "But tell you what--since you are always a stubborn-ass nigger, Buck, you going to keep working until the morning. Night, you can go to bed now."

Night stood motionless. He hated to leave Buck to do all that work on his own. He knew how tired they both were.

"Okay nigger, you do not want to move," Master Carter got down off his horse.

"You want to stay and help your fellow monkey."

Allen knew that he and Night could take out Master Carter. Allen also remembered that Master Carter released Jake and David, his two overseers, at 8:00pm that night. He was alone now. The overseers lived within walking distance from the big house. Master Carter was a small, frail man; barely five feet tall. He stood protected behind his gun and his whip, and of course, his white skin. If they were to attack him they would have to kill him and bury him fast enough that no one would hear. That would give them time to run away. Master pulled out his pistol and pointed it right at Night's face.

"I ought to blast your gorilla face right off nigger, but I cannot afford to lose good chattel. Stay and help Buck then."

As soon as Master Carter turned around to walk back to his horse, Allen picked up his axe and swung it; splitting Master Carter's head wide open. The blows happened so fast that there were no screams--just instant death. The lights had gone out permanently for Mr. Carter.

Night could not believe his eyes. Master Carter stood motionless for a second, and then dropped to his knees.

"You killed Master. Are you trying to get us all killed?" said Night.

"Killed? Are you a fool or what?! What type of life is this--we might as well be dead! I am trying to get us free! I mean, the beatings, the lynching's, working yourself to death and nothing to show for it. This man raped your wife; you remember that. She has had two children from him. He sold your daughter off to God knows where."

Night was speechless as he contemplated everything that Allen had just told him.

"Help me bury this bastard," said Allen.

The two men pulled the body deep into the woods. They buried Master Carter's body and put some of the wood they had chopped on top of the gravesite to disguise it.

"Now what?" asked Night?

"We run, that's what. Go gather the other slaves; tell them they're free and to run. Get Solomon first, he always talks of running away and how he has connections with abolitionists. We need to speak with him as soon as possible, but I guarantee there are some snitches amongst them. Gather who you can trust; I'll deal with Master's wife."

Allen ran across the huge plantation to the big house. There was a female slave, fairly light, almost white in complexion, sweeping the porch as he approached.

"Boy, Master know you coming up on this porch? Now you know y'all dark niggers don't come near the Big House," she said as she stood in front of the door.

"Master's dead."

"What!!" she screamed.

Allen pushed her out of his way. Then he barged in. The Master's house was beautiful inside. Allen did not look too long, but went straight up to the bedroom. He looked through the crack of the door. There she was in the mirror combing her hair. Allen opened the door.

"Buck, what the hell are you doing?! My husband will kill you."

"Your husband is no more. Get up." She took a whip from her husband's dresser drawer.

"Get back, boy," she said. Allen smacked her, and she fell to the floor.

Allen screamed for her to get up. He took her out of the house. The plantation was in an uproar. Some slaves were running for freedom, while others were too scared to run. Allen took her outside and then called all the slaves up in the middle of the field. Allen had Master's pistol in one hand and his wife in the other. Wilma was in fear for her life.

"Look, Master is dead. So time is short; if you want freedom, run now." Night stood there next to his brother, Solomon, and his family. "Solomon, guide the slaves towards that abolitionist that you said lives near."

"That's over a 50-mile walk," said Solomon.

"Take time to plan. An hour or so, then we run," said Allen. We will use the horses as well.

Allen then spoke to all the slave women.

"Here's Wilma, the woman that beat some of you half to death for now working hard or fast enough. Have your way with her." Allen walked away. Shortly he heard Wilma's scream as several slave girls attacked her.

Allen found Night and his family waiting at his shack. They got their belongings and headed for freedom with Solomon as the guide. Night told Allen that at least four slaves went to tell what had happened. Allen knew the overseers and bounty hunters would be on the way to get the plantation back in order and take control of the slaves. Allen, Night, and his family were now on the run through the woods.

After 3 hours temperature had dropped. It was cold, and they were hungry. They took some food, but it did not last long. They made sure that Night's children and wife ate first. Allen could not believe what was happening. It was as if he was living someone else's life.

Two days had passed since they had made their escape for freedom. Allen was asleep along with Night's family, while Night stood guard. He stood in the darkness, pacing back and forth. Night was so fearful of getting captured. He knew the penalty would be death for him and his family, but it felt good not to be breaking his back working all day, as he had been doing for his entire life. Seeing his wife rest as he stood guard felt good; she deserved it. He prayed that they would make it to freedom.

After four weeks of following the North Star, and watching the direction of the sun, the slaves made it to the North. They settled in Philadelphia, Pennsylvania. During their long trip they had allured bounty hunters several times, hiding in homes of abolitionists, and at times deep in the woodland where they nearly starved to death. Night had a brother who was a free man, and he planned to find him. In the meantime, they stayed at a local abolitionist's house, a man named Mr. Parker. He planned to help Allen and Night find jobs. Allen felt surely this was his new life.

Late one evening before he went the bed, Allen prayed to God.

"God, I know throughout my life I have made mistakes, especially the most egregious mistake of being a racist. Please bless my family and touch all of them let them know that discriminating against other people because of the color of their skin is wrong. God, please make right the wrong I have set on them. And touch my oldest son Kevin. Let him know I love him, and that he was right for not following what I tried to impose on him. God, I have accepted this new life you have given me as Buck, a black man. I have learned a lot, and I thank you for it. Amen."

When Allen opened his eyes, he saw a little girl standing in front of him. He was startled for a second.

"Hey, are you lost, little lady?" said Allen.

"No, but you used to be," said the girl. "My name is Estella. I know your son James."

Allen could not believe his ears.

"Is he okay? Is my family okay?"

"Yes, they miss you very much. I'm the little girl you son often tried to tell you about, but you and the rest of the family did not believe him. When he mentioned seeing slaves working on a plantation he was telling the truth. I was a slave on your great, great, great, grandfather's plantation. He lived in the house you live in now. I came to your son to show him the world of slavery, so he would not become an evil man like you once were. He is a good boy. I am here to let you know that God has heard your prayer."

"So you're a ghost. And the man that--" She cut Allen off.

"That man was my grandpa. I told him to show you as much as he could about slavery in hopes it would change you. I'm glad that everything worked out." said Estella.

"What about me? Is this my life?" Estella reached out her hand.

"Come with me." The two walked toward the bedroom door and when they opened it there was a bright light. Before Allen stepped through the door he asked, "What about Night and his family?"

"They will be fine. And so will Buck," she said.

"What do you mean?"

"You were living his life. He was a courageous man; after his freedom he became an abolitionist. He even started a newspaper once he learned to read. To help fight for freedom."

Allen bent down and kissed the little girl on the cheek.

"Thank you, Estella. Let me say goodbye to Night," he said.

Allen ran to Night's room. Night was startled when Allen burst through his door and stood up, rifle in hand. He was still on edge after fleeing from slavery.

"What's wrong with you, Buck, I almost shot you!" Night and his family were in the room cooking dinner.

"I am sorry, Night. I have to go. I am leaving," said Allen.

"Man, we just got here. I know the place is small but it's better than the shacks on Master Carter's plantation," stated Night.

"Yes, Night, you're right. This is hard to explain. I have a family too that I must return to," said Allen. Night put down his rifle and embraced Allen.

"I understand; this life as a slave was a tough road. Many families are torn apart. I still want to find my other children one day soon. To think I may die and not see them again is not good." Night took a necklace from his neck.

89

"This will give you peace and strength along your journey," said Night. Night's family each hugged Allen, and thanked him for helping lead them to freedom.

Allen left Night's room as Estella waited in the Hall. Estella reached for Allen's hand. The two headed towards the front door. Estella opened the door and again the bright light appeared. The two stepped through the door.

Chapter 11

In moments, Allen was in front of his home. He could not believe his eyes. He looked down to thank Estella once again, but she was gone. Allen walked toward his house. He looked at his clothes. He was back in the same slacks and shirt and tie he had on when he left. He felt his neck to find that the necklace Night had given him was still there. Allen ran to his front door, but inside no one was home. Tiffany and the children had stepped out to the grocery store. Allen went in through the patio door, since it was usually open. He looked around his home.

The first thing he did would be taken down the rebel flag and painting of Robert E. Lee that hung in his living room. Allen was prepared to make a complete 180-degree change. Soon, he heard the car pull up. Allen watched from the window as his family got out of the car. Tiffany got to the door first. When she opened the door and saw Allen standing there she dropped her bags and fainted. Allen quickly revived her as his children screamed in joy.

"I knew you'd come back," said Jenny.

"I told you mommy," said James. Soon Tiffany came to here senses. "Honey, I missed you so much. Why did you leave us? I thought you loved me." "I do, and that's why I'm here now for good."

"Where were you?" his wife asked.

"It's a long story. Come on in, guys. I'm starving."

The family sat down for dinner. Tiffany invited Langston and Christina over too. Everyone had so many questions, but Allen did not tell them everything.

"So where did you go, bro," asked Langston.

"Yeah, come on Dad," added Kevin.

"I was under a lot of stress at work. I had to get away. I needed to clear my head." Allen looked at James and quickly winked his right eye. James smiled.

"Enough with all the questions; let's eat."

Later that night while in bed Tiffany demanded to know where he had gone, but Allen stuck to the same story. In the back of her mind she wondered if it was another woman. As his wife kept demanding to know where he had been for the past couple of months, Allen got out of the bed and looked out the window.

"All you need to know is that there are about to be some changes. I was wrong all those years, teaching all of you to hate blacks. I hope you and Jenny can change. Kevin never caught on to it, thank God, and James was too young to understand."

"Are you serious, honey?" "I never really was racist. I kind of just assumed it was right." "I mean, my parents and your parents taught us to be this way."

"I know, honey, but the chain breaks here. And I'm going to tell Langston; maybe he and Christina will be influenced as well. Langston always followed whatever I said or did. He should listen. I put racism in his head more than our parents did. I must make it right now."

"Honey, why the sudden change?" asked his wife.

"It needs to be done," he said. Allen laid down in the bed. After some long awaited passionate sex, the couple was soon fast asleep.

Allen was up early the next day. He went into James's room to wake his son. He sat on the edge of the bed.

"Dad," said the little boy, still half asleep.

"Hello son. I just want you to know I'm sorry for not believing you."

"I met Estella and her grandpa."

"They changed my life."

"She told me about you."

"You're a good boy. You will be a great father and husband one day. I will make sure of that."

"Dad, have you changed?"

"Yes, son, everything Estella showed you and I, what happened to African Americans during slavery, it delivered me. I was wrong for trying to make my family hate other races and cultures. From this day forth I will not rest until I make things right. Go ahead and get some more sleep, son, I know it's early." Allen kissed his son on the head.

The next day Allen took his two oldest children out to eat while Tiffany stayed home with James. Allen wanted to be alone with the two children to tell them about his new way of life.

"Dad, why are we doing this? We usually all go out and eat as a family," said Jenny.

Kevin sat there simply listing to his iPod. He had no idea what his father was going to tell him. Allen signaled to Kevin to take off his headphones.

"Listen kids, I know I have been hard on you guys with my views on other races of people. But I want you to know is that I was wrong. I went through some things in my life that made me the way I used to be. And now, as of recently, I have experienced some new things that have changed who I was. If you have not already noticed I took down all the Civil War stuff I had up. Jenny, it may be hard, but try your best to change your ways. It's wrong to be racist, and Kevin, thank God my ways never affected you. Keep being the way you are."

"Dad, I thought being like the way you taught me was right. The majority of my friends are like, well, racist, but we do have some black friends."

"Look Jenny change your ways. If your friends cannot accept it, then get new friends."

Jenny was puzzled, but at the same time she knew her dad meant well. Kevin stood up and embraced his dad in tears. He was so happy his dad had made a change. The family ate their food and talked for a bit. Allen had missed out on quality time since his absence. Kevin told his father about his girlfriend Daesha, and that she was black. His father told him as long as she treats him right, color did not matter. Kevin could not wait to tell Daesha the news.

Allen had a lot more work to do. He was going to keep his promise to God to try and change people he affected by racism. Allen had planned to try and tracked down the most recent people he had affected. Allen felt that he should also confront Todd, the rookie lawyer he had made racial slurs about. Tiffany thought Allen was crazy when he said he was going to New York to make peace with Todd, but after she realized how sincere he was, she understood.

Allen left for New York early that Sunday Morning. He stayed at Glen's house, a partner from his law firm. Glen was glad to see Allen. The two men talked and joked about old times in law school at NYU.

"So, are you thinking about coming back to the Big Apple?" said Glen.

93

"Well, the thought has crossed my mind. The firm is doing so well that I can pretty much retire any time now, and I have invested hundreds of thousands. Money is no object, but I have changed, man." said Allen.

"What are you talking about?"

" You and I built this law firm, but we did it the wrong way. I'm not a racist anymore. I do not view people of different backgrounds the way I used to. I know we built our firm on the good old boy, redneck way, but it has to change."

"Hey man, this sudden change--why now? Don't forget Mr. Marshall is a good old boy to the heart, and he owns more of the firm than we do."

"I know you're not going to go to him with this."

"This could destroy us," said Glen. "We made a small effort in 20 years. We just hired our first black lawyer.

"That's ridiculous," said Allen.

"Todd quit a little after you left. Mr. Marshall did not want to tell you. He figured you would worry about a lawsuit. Equal Opportunity says we must hire more minorities, and Mr. Marshall is in an uproar," said Glen.

"Look Glen, I am asking you to consider changing your bigoted ways, and even if I have to do it alone, I will try and change this firm that we helped build."

Allen left Glen's house and checked into the Hilton.

On Monday morning he met with Mr. Marshall and other leaders of the Firm. They were under the impression that Allen was doing a report on cases at the southern office. Little did they know they were in for a rude awakening. When Allen walked in the room there was complete silence. After listening to various conversations around the room, Allen cleared his voice.

"Hello, ladies and gentlemen. This Law firm has grossed millions over the years. I'm proud to be a co-founder of The Thomas & Marshall Law firm. I also thank Mr. Marshall who came on as a co-owner two years after I started the company, and for letting my name stay first on the building." The room of lawyers chuckled.

"I want to apologize for my absence at the southern branch of the firm over the past couple of months. I was under the weather and stressed, so I took a vacation, I guess you could say. I did not even tell my family. I'm lucky to still have a wife. She is a good woman. I also apologize for numbers dropping in our Virginia office, but what I'm getting at is change. Change is good."

"What kind of change, may I ask, are we doing?" said Mr. Marshall.

"I know we're all making well over six figures," said Allen. Once again, the room of lawyers laughed.

"But it's not all about money. I want this company to be about ethics, values, and principals. Our values and principals have not been the best. Let's face it: I will be blunt," Allen paused.

"Racism! That's who I used to be and who the majority of you are, and what the firm has been built on." Allen could sense uneasiness in the room amongst the lawyers.

"Most of you all may not be really racist, but still play along with it knowing you are not that way but you have car payments, mortgages, getaway homes, and your children's student loans, so you go along with the racial jokes, and trying to keep it an allwhite law firm. I heard Todd left. I'm sure he was driven away. And I'm no saint; I participated in the antics. I was the ringleader, some may say. But I have changed and I ask you to change. Now I know it will not be over night. But let's put forth the effort." Allen paused.

"Well, I'm finished." Allen walked away from the podium.

"Allen, I want to see you in my office as soon as possible," said Mr. Marshall.

Allen did not know what to expect. Allen walked in the office with him.

"Who the hell do you think you are: Jesus Christ? Are you trying to save the world?" asked Mr. Marshall

"No I'm not, sir, I just made a change."

"Look, I fronted you more than half of the three hundred thousand you needed to build this law firm. Technically, I'm the real owner and everyone knows that. I also own more shares of the company's, and the apps and website."

I'm not changing my ways for you or anyone else. You're not going to take this firm down because you had a sudden change of heart," said Mr. Marshall.

"Look," stated Allen.

"Look my ass, Allen."

"Wake up: this is how it is. It's too late for changes. If you do not want to conform to the way this law firm has always been then I'm going to have to let you go."

"I quit!" yelled Allen. Oh, and I will have the equal opportunity and the NAACP investigate this firm immediately! Not to mention the Better Business Bureau and the New York Bar!"

Allen slammed the door on the way out. Most of the lawyers from the meeting were in the hallway listening. They looked at Allen in pity, but not one spoke a word to him except for Glen.

Glen walked Allen downstairs.

"Man, it's hard when people are stuck in their ways. I respect you for making this change and risking your job. I wish I had the balls."

"Just tell me where Todd works," said Allen.

"He is at "U need a Lawyer," a small firm in Queens," said Glen. The two men embraced.

"I will be okay. Think about your life and the people you have affected by racism."

Allen walked off and shook his head. He was out of a job from a firm he helped build, but it would be better this way. Allen did not want to be around bigots anyway.

Next, he tracked down Todd and apologized to him face to face. Todd shook Allen's hand. He told Allen he wished more people in the world were willing to make a change. The two men had lunch and talked an hour or so. Todd even asked Allen for his resume to help him get another job, but Allen told him maybe he would take a break from practicing law.

Chapter 12

Allen was deep in thought during his plane ride back to Virginia. How would he tell his family he had lost his job? Was it worth it, he thought, changing his life this late in the game? He was in his mid-forties. Deep inside Allen knew God let this thing happen to him for a reason. Estella and her grandpa came into his and his youngest son's life for a reason.

After an hour and a half on the plane, Allen was back home. He picked up his car from the airport parking lot, then drove to the park where he had lost his first love. Allen looked at the tennis courts where the real-life nightmare had taken place. Allen walked through the park, then sat on a bench in deep thought. Where was his life headed now? He had close to a million saved in bonds and retirement accounts. That would suffice for a bit, he thought. Allen finally got enough heart to go face his family, and tell them the bad news. As he approached his car, his cellphone rang.

"Hello, Allen Speaking."

"Yes, Allen, this is Mr. Marshall. Just in case that brother of yours gets a change of heart I've decided to let him go too."

"But sir, he has a family."

"Yeah, you were family with this firm. Put away your Good Samaritan act and you can come back to the good old days and your job. The offer stands, and your brother will still have a job."

Allen was in a difficult situation. He would be supporting racism if he returned to work at the firm. Allen promised God and Estella he would make a change, but at the same time, his brother's career was on the line. Allen assumed his brother had money stashed away for a rainy day. And if not, he would help.

"Sir I will pass on that." Allen hung up the phone.

Now on top of telling his family the news, Allen had to tell his brother this bad news. Allen pulled up slowly to his brother's house. Langston was sitting on the porch reading the newspaper.

"Hey, what's going on man?" "Nothing much," said Allen.

"How did the end of the year meeting go? I'm sorry I could not make it man. Both the kids had the flu."

"Don't worry, Langston, it's okay. We need to talk. You know how we were raised."

"Yeah, what do you mean, though?"

"You know, to hate other races of people, especially blacks. Well I've changed. And I have been working on my family."

"What the hell man, don't tell me you are preaching that race shit to me. It's a part of my life now."

"Just listen!" yelled Allen.

"So let me get this straight: now you want me to change my ways? What about the firm? Damn near everyone we hired, and the big boss Marshall are good old boys. Mr. Marshall would flip."

"Look, it's up to you to change. We cannot hate a person because of the color of their skin. No one knows what race they are when they are born until someone tells them. Children play together regardless of race. We make that separation. And as for the firm, Mr. Marshall fired me," said Allen.

"What! See, that's what I mean. Think about your family. Now you have to find another job." Allen looked at his younger brother. He put his hand on Langston's shoulder.

"He fired you too Langston. Mr. Marshall felt as though you'd have a change of heart too." Langston tossed his newspaper that he was reading.

"What the fuck man! My bills, the mortgage, car notes! Did you think about your family? Get the fuck off my porch!"

"Langston, calm down," said Allen.

"You're not wanted here anymore, Allen." said Langston, as he entered his house, slamming the door behind him.

Allen shook his head and walked away. In Allen's heart he knew he could not be the man he used to be. It just was not in him. Estella had changed his life. He wished others could understand him and his change. Although he was being labeled as the bad guy now, Allen had peace of mind and that's what mattered to him. Knowing that, he had made a change for the good.

It was late evening as Allen approached his screen door, dreading the reaction he would get from his family, especially his wife. She was just getting over his being gone nearly three months. Everyone was home. James was in the living room putting together a puzzle. Kevin and Jenny, argued over the T.V., as usual. His wife Tiffany was in the kitchen with Daesha, Kevin's girlfriend, helping to prepare dinner.

"Hey everyone," called Allen. Tiffany jumped up and ran and hugged Allen tight. She kissed him several times. She felt weird every time he left the house now, still a little fearful she would lose him again.

"So how did the meeting go?" asked Jenny.

"Yes honey, tell us all about it." Allen froze up.

"It was okay. You know, some changes for the New Year are in progress." Then Allen quickly changed the subject.

"So, let's go out to eat."

"But honey, I cooked," said Tiffany.

"Yeah but we need more family time together."

Allen took the family to Red Lobster. The family loved seafood. Through the night all Allen could think of was how he would tell his wife and family he was no longer employed. After dinner when everyone was in bed asleep, Allen was wide awoke. He gazed at the ceiling fan for hours. What had he done, he thought. What if Marshall blackballed him and he could not practice as a lawyer anywhere? The mortgage, college funds, and other expenses, etc. all kinds of things ran through his head. On top of that his own brother had disowned him. Allen knew he would have to tell his family soon. If Tiffany talked to Christina, then the truth would surely come out. Allen decided he would tell his wife the news in the morning and break the news to the kids later in the day.

Allen was the first one up that morning, having not really slept much that night, and he prepared breakfast. Tiffany had the day off (most of the time Tiffany slept late on her days off, even though she was still on call at the hospital). Allen ate breakfast with the kids. He even threw on a suit to avoid answering any questions from the kids. After the children left out for school, Allen brewed some coffee. His wife loved coffee first thing in the morning. Instead of turning to Fox News as he always did in the mornings, Allen watched CNN as he waited for his wife to come down stairs. As soon as Tiffany smelled the coffee she awoke and came downstairs.

"Hey honey, are you going in late today?" Allen handed her a cup of coffee. "I need to talk to you, baby."

"What's on your mind?" said Tiffany as she took a sip.

"The meeting in New York." Allen paused a second or two.

"It did not go as planned."

"Mr. Marshall did not appreciate my changing my ways on being a racist, and not to mention the rest of the good old boys that I helped hire. I was fired."

Tiffany's cup of coffee dropped to the floor. The cup shattered.

"Honey, what do you mean fired? Were you even thinking about your family?"

"Look, I cannot surround myself with people that are racist if I have chosen not to be that way anymore. They fired Langston too. And he does not want anything to do with me," said Allen.

"Is it really worth it? You could have faked it just to stay employed. I do not make enough to pay our bills. And how will I explain to my colleagues that my husband was fired from a law firm he built? You have always been the breadwinner," said Tiffany as she stormed off.

"Where are you going?" asked Allen.

"I can't take this. First you leave your family for three months, maybe with some woman, now this. I'm gathering my things and moving in with my mom."

Allen stormed out of the house, got in his car and drove off. He had no idea where he was going. His own wife was turning against him, not to mention his brother. All he had now were his children. And what if they took sides, he thought to himself. Allen went to the liquor store and bought a bottle of Jack Daniels. He then drove to a Wal-Mart parking lot and began to drink the liquor like it was water.

Suddenly Allen heard a voice.

"You have done the right thing."

He looked in the back seat. It was Estella.

"Not many people make a change in their life, especially one that will affect their life and others." said Estella.

"But my family hates me now I have lost my job. My own Brother turned his back on me. I mean, I cannot change the world."

"I promise you your change was for the best. Come with me." Estella got out of the car. Allen left his bottle and followed.

"And you will not be gone long this time." said Estella with a laugh.

The two headed into the woods behind Walmart. Then suddenly they were inside of a house. It was Allen's house. Allen and Estella stood in the living room. There was an old man sitting in a chair reading the paper.

"That old man is you, sir." said Estella. The old man was crying. "You have not heard from your son Kevin since he left for college seven years ago. He does not want anything to do with you because you never accepted him not being racist, and you did not accept his wife Daesha. You have not seen or heard from him in years." The old man got up and looked out the window.

"A car is coming up the road honey, it's Kevin." said the old man.

"It's not him. He's never coming here, okay; get it through your head, Allen," said Tiffany.

Estella grabbed Allen's hand and they walked out of the house. The two were back in the Walmart parking lot.

"Family is the most important thing. My father was lynched, and my two sisters and brother were sold off to owners of different plantations. I know it seems bad now but it could be worse. God choose you for a reason. You cannot change the world but try and change some people, okay?"

Estella faded away. As quickly as she had come, she was gone. Allen now stood alone. He walked back to the car. Allen drove to a nearby motel, got a room and passed out, drunk from the bottle of Jack Daniels.

Chapter 13

Allen had a hangover from hell. It was 9 am and checkout time was in a couple of hours. Allen did not know what to expect when he got home. He was pretty sure his wife had told the kids the news. Allen sat in the chair looking out the window and finally convinced himself to go home. When Allen got to the house, Kevin was in the kitchen cooking.

"Hey Dad, what's going on? Mom told us about the job and all." "I figured she would," said Allen.

"Jenny and mom left; they went to stay with Grandma Helen."

"Where's James?" asked Allen. "He is asleep in his room. Jenny took it hard. She is not open-minded at all. The influence you put on the family is hard to break. I argued with her and mom for hours yesterday before they left, but I could not win," said Kevin.

"At least I have you and James. I'm very sad that it came to this, but it is for the best. We'll be blessed in the long run," said Allen as he embraced his son.

Allen went to the drawer in his office desk. He pulled out a bottle of Wild Turkey. He poured a glass that was equivalent to four shots. Allen sat at the desk.

"Lord, I'm out of a job; my wife left; my brother disowned me; what now? I feel I've done the right thing---I mean, I know I have." Tears ran down Allen's face.

He drank until he was drunk. He had locked the door to his office.

Kevin tried several times to get in to check on his father throughout the evening, but each time Allen told his son to go away and that he would be out soon. Allen had an old bottle of muscle relaxers that he was given some time ago when he had a back injury; he had never used them all. Allen stared at the bottle for some time. Finally, he emptied it into his glass. He also emptied a bottle of Oxycodone in to the bottle. Allen felt he had nothing else to live for. He had made the change for the best but it still seemed to him he was being

punished in the end. Maybe it was because of all the wrong doing he did to minorities throughout his life. Allen crushed up all the pills together until it was a fine powder he poured in the rest of the wild turkey into the glass, stirred it up with his desk pen, and drank it. Almost immediately he regretted doing it right as he regretted, he felt side effects. Minutes later he began to shake furiously and foamed at the mouth. He fell out of his chair. Kevin woke up his little brother they went down stairs to see was all the commotion about. Kevin screamed for his father. But all he heard was moaning. Kevin kicked in the door, to find his father laid out on the floor, still foaming at the mouth.

"Dad, get up please," he yelled with tears in his eyes. James stared from the doorway in fear.

"Go get the phone, hurry," Kevin yelled to his little brother. Kevin held his father as he shook.

Allen's eyes rolled back into his head. He whispered to his son.

"I love you, your mom, and your siblings. I'm sorry." James

gave his brother the phone.

When the ambulance arrived, Allen was pronounced dead on the scene. By that time, Tiffany and Jenny had arrived. The family was in disbelief. Allen Thomas was gone.

The Thomas family moved back to New York a year later. Tiffany got her old job back. She had changed in her views on African Americans and other races. After her husband's death she realized how badly he had wanted the family to change. It was gradual, but it was a change. Jenny also changed; she separated herself from friends that were racist. Jenny knew that separating herself from others that were racist would be key in her change. Kevin went off to an art college where he reunited with his best friend Derrick. He stayed in touch with Daesha; she attended St. John's University, so the two were not far apart. They continued their relationship. Kevin always reminded his family of the importance of accepting all races and not stereotyping them. He was determined to change everyone he met that was racist. James was now in middle school. He missed his father and often cried himself to sleep at night. He sometimes wished Estella would come and visit him.

As for Estella, she is still living in the Thomas house as she has for many years. At night her spirit roams throughout the hallways of the house. She often goes into James's room wishing he was there. She knew that she could not visit him in New York. Her job was to warn anyone who moved into the Thomas house about the harsh life of slavery, even if it meant bringing them into that harsh life of slavery first hand. Some fifteen years had passed. One morning she noticed a white family walking up to the house.

"Honey this is it: our dream house. I cannot believe they're letting it go for the price the realtor told me," said a woman.

"And there are no blacks, or Mexicans in this area too thank God. Finally, an area we can raise our kids away from those gangbangers and thugs", said the man to his fiancé as they walked into the house.

Estella smiled. Finally, it was time to go back to work.

The end.

People like Malcolm X, Martin Luther King, John Brown, and Medgar Evers fought for our civil rights to end racism, and even gave their lives. We must educate our children, and stop teaching racism to our youth. Our youth are the future. Let's work with them to make a better America with equal opportunities for all races of mankind. I hope this book touches everyone who reads it.